# Hating JAMIE JACKSON

## JESSICA MADDEN

**ISBN:** 978-0-646-87933-8

*For the writing community who helped me to keep writing until I found my inspiration*

# Chapter One

I didn't know what was worse. Slipping on a patch of ice, or being wracked with so much force by a snowball, that it startles you, making you slip on ice and land on your back with half of the school witnessing. I wanted to believe that slipping on the patch of ice on the path leading to the front entrance of the school was embarrassing, as slipping on ice was a normal thing to do. But no. It wasn't the ice that sent me flying to the ground. The snowball is what startled me, which then causes me to slip.

Allegra, my best friend, gasps. "Candice, are you alright? Are you hurt?"

I lie there for a few seconds, staring up at her, trying to feel any kind of pain from hitting the ground hard. I expected my back to hurt, or even my head. Did I hit my head? I don't remember.

"I don't think I'm hurt," I answer.

And then I hear it, the ball of laughter coming from the

direction of the where the snowball had been thrown.

"Good one, Jackson!" I hear one of the guys call out.

I narrow my eyes at the name. I bolt upright, ignoring the hand Allegra had held out to help me back on my feet. I glance over at the guys from the ice hockey team, laughing at me like this was the funniest thing ever. Among the group was no doubt the biggest jerk in the entire school, Jamie Jackson.

Why did it not surprise me that the jerk was the one who had thrown the snowball my way? It was like he enjoyed annoying me. Ever since kindergarten, he found ways to get under my skin.

I get to my feet, and our eyes meet across the lawn. He had a huge grin on his face, his brown eyes lit up, like he was so proud of bringing me down and embarrassing me in front of everyone.

Jamie held up his hand, the grin never leaving his face. "Sorry, O'Connor. My bad."

I clench my fist. Damn right it was his bad. And no, he isn't sorry.

Allegra takes my arm, pulling me away before I do something I was going to regret. Like stomping across the lawn and standing face to face with Jamie Jackson, ready to give him a piece of my mind. It's probably a good thing she stopped me because I would mostly make an even bigger fool out of myself.

We walk through the doors of the building, being greeted by the warm heater.

"Can you believe that jerk?" I shake my head, making my way past the office and down the corridor leading to my locker.

Allegra walks alongside me, struggling to keep up as I walk fast. "I'm sure Jamie didn't do it on purpose."

I laugh. "That would be the day. He totally did it on purpose. What did he think he would get out of hitting me with the snowball? I should report him to the principal and then have snowball fights banned."

"Hey, don't be one of those people to ruin the fun for everyone. You don't want everyone hating on you because you banned snowball fights. We are one of the only schools in this area that still allows them."

"There's a difference between having fun and doing it on purpose. And Jamie *did* it on purpose."

I reach my locker, putting in my combination, and opening it. I glance at the mirror I had hanging on the door, checking to see if the silver stud on my nose was still there. It was. If it had fallen out because of Jamie, I would have killed him. Sure, that nose piercing got me in all sorts of trouble when I got it without my parents' permission a couple of months ago, but I would hate to have anything happen to it.

"Look, after today, it's winter break and you don't have to deal with him for two weeks," Allegra points out. "Just think that you will be spending Christmas and the New Year in Rocky Springs. Jamie will be nowhere in sight."

I nod. I know Allegra was right, but it honestly didn't feel like she was. "I rather be away from him longer than two weeks."

Allegra gives me a small smile. "I know. And I'm still jealous you're going to Colorado for Christmas. I would love to spend Christmas in the Rocky Mountains. It seems like the perfect destination to spend Christmas."

Rather than spending Christmas here in Parkerville, New York, my parents thought it would be great for our family to spend it in Colorado. Rocky Springs was a small ski resort town, not far from Aspen. I couldn't wait to spend Christmas there.

"I wish you could come too. Maybe next winter break we can take a trip there, just the two of us, and share all our stories about college."

Allegra smiles at me. "That sounds great, Candice."

The bell rings then. I quickly grab my English and math books from my locker. Together, Allegra and I head off to homeroom.

The first subject of the day was English. I loved English, but Jamie Jackson made me hate it. Allegra and I take a seat in the centre of the classroom. I keep my head down when the jerk walks through the door with his idiotic friends.

Someone stands in front of my desk. I didn't have to look up to see that the jeans and the red, blue, and white Rangers jersey belong to none other than Jamie Jackson.

I look up at him, crossing my arms across my chest, and raise an eyebrow at him. "What do you want?"

He chuckles. "It seems like someone woke up on the wrong side of the bed this morning."

"Really? Well, it seems like you woke up as a jerk this morning. Oh wait, no. You do that every day."

Jamie put his hands on the table and leans in closer to me. "Listen, about this morning. I'm really sorry about hitting you with the snowball. I swear it wasn't supposed to hit you. I wasn't even aiming at you."

I scoff. "Yeah, you aren't sorry."

Before he could say anything in response, Mrs. Hadley walks into the classroom. That was Jamie's cue to walk away and take a seat. He takes his spot in the back. I keep my eyes to the front so I don't see that jerk. I'm thankful he isn't in my math class next period. But I do have biology and home economics with him later on. I just want the day to be over so I don't have to see his face.

\* \* \*

I had a clear view of Jamie over at the jocks' table at lunch today. But Jamie wasn't the person I had my eye on. My sixteen-year-old sister, Gabriella, was standing near them, talking. She had a clipboard in her hand and I wonder what the jocks are saying to her. I can see the cheerleaders making fun of her appearance. Gabriella pushes the glasses up on the bridge of her nose.

"How can the jocks sit there and say nasty stuff to people and get away with it?" I ask Allegra, who sat across from me.

Allegra looks over where I was glancing at. She turns back to me. "I don't know. But I'm sure your sister can handle them. Gabriella is smart."

I knew she was smart. She was a straight A student, and does tutoring on the side. She had tutored a few of the jocks. But I wasn't worried about how smart she was. It was the bullying. Gabriella pretty much kept to herself, and didn't tell our parents about the bullying that goes on in school. Mostly kids tease her about being smart. I saw her get laughed at a few times, and I tell her to stand up for herself, but she tells me she is okay and she can handle it. I hope she can. I worry how she will handle her senior year once I go off to college next year.

Gabriella eventually moved away from the jock table when she realized that she wasn't going to get through to them with whatever she wanted. She spots me, and I wave to her. She smiles, making her way over to our table. Past her shoulder, I saw Jamie glance our way. I ignore him the best I can.

My sister stands next to Allegra. She gives us a small smile. "Hey."

I point towards the jock table with my fork, which I should be using to eat my chicken salad, but I was too busy focusing on the jocks. "They aren't giving you a hard time, are they?"

Gabriella glances over at the table before turning back to me. "Don't worry about it, Candice."

For someone who was a genius, Gabriella really didn't know how to stand up to herself when it came to bullying.

I shake my head. "No, Gabriella. Don't let those jerks walk over you. Stand up to them, okay?"

She nods, but something in her dark brown eyes told me that she wasn't going to do it. I knew that once again I had to march myself over there to say something to them. And I really didn't want to go over there where that jerk face Jamie Jackson was. I won't be happy if he had said anything nasty about my sister. I don't care if he says nasty stuff to me, I just don't want him saying it to my sister.

Before my sister or Allegra could stop me, I stood up and walk over to the jock table.

Chelsea Chamberlain looks up at me when I approach them. "Well, it looks like another O'Connor sister is coming over. Are you lost?" She points over at my table. "I believe your table is over there."

I stand there, looking around at them all – the cheerleaders and the star athletes of Parkerville High. But mostly my eyes were on Jamie, wondering what sarcastic comment he will say to me.

"Whatever you guys were saying to my sister, stop it," I warn them. "If you want to call her nasty names, say them to me. She doesn't need you to be so awful to her."

"Relax, Candice," Chad Logan says to me. "We were just chatting with her."

"It didn't look like it was from where I was sitting."

I look at Jamie, waiting for him to say something.

His lips curl into a smirk. "Were you adopted?"

I stare at him. Why on earth was he bringing that up all of a sudden? "What?"

"Were you adopted?"

"Why are you asking me that question?"

Jamie shrugs. "Just curious because you and Gabriella don't look like sisters. I mean, your hair is red and your eyes are blue. Your sister has light brown hair and brown eyes."

I narrow my eyes at him. Of course he would ask me a dumb question like that. I inherited my father's red hair and blue eyes, while Gabriella and my nine-years-old sister, Hannah, inherited Mom's light brown hair and brown eyes.

"No, I wasn't adopted, you jerk. My dad has red hair too, okay?"

He shrugs. "Fair enough."

Chelsea points to my table. "Okay, can you go now? The loser table is over there."

I wanted to say something else, but I figured I better not. So I turn and head back to my table.

"What did they say?" Allegra asks me.

"Can you believe that jerk face Jamie asked me if I'm adopted?" I answer.

Allegra's eyes widen. "Jamie said that?"

"Yeah, he did. You know just because I'm a redhead and Gabriella isn't, doesn't mean I'm adopted." I shake my head.

Gabriella grips her clipboard. "Don't worry about what

they say, Candice. They are just bored and have nothing better to say about anyone."

I agree to this.

"Anyway, I was over there talking to them because Miss Fields asked me to go around to students to ask if anyone would like to volunteer with helping decorating the winter dance at the end of next month. The dance community has already come up with a theme, now they just need volunteers to help with decorations when the time comes to do so."

"And what did they say?" I nod towards the jock table.

Gabriella looks over her shoulder at them before she turns back to Allegra and me. "The cheerleaders think they don't have to help out with anything." She holds out the clipboard to us. "Would you guys like to put your name down? Miss Fields is also holding a meeting in the gym this afternoon."

I smile at my sister. "Sure. Why not?"

Gabriella smiles and hands me the clipboard. I write my name on the list. Allegra also signs up.

"Thank you so much, guys," Gabriella says before walking away.

I went back to my salad. I only took a couple of bites before I said, "You know, one of these days, Jamie is going to be sorry for what he said to me, as well as for the other things he has done."

"Let's not talk about him right now, and finish our lunch, okay?" Allegra suggests.

But I didn't want to eat my lunch. I wanted to complain about Jamie because that's what I always do. I honestly could write a book about why I hated that stupid jerk so much.

The rest of the day went by fast, and I managed to get through my classes with him in them. I keep my focus on my work so I didn't have to face him. Just glancing his way for a moment will only cause the irritation to grow, and I didn't want to do that in the middle of class.

At the end of the day, instead of racing towards the exit to celebrate winter break, Allegra and I made our way to the gym. Several students from different grades were there. Gabriella stood beside Miss Fields near the bleachers, along with two students from the dance committee. Gabriella smiles and waves at me. I return the wave, and then sat on the third row of the bleachers with Allegra.

Just as Miss Fields, the art teacher here at Parkerville High, was about to speak, the last student arrives, his bag swinging over his shoulder. As soon as I lay my eyes on him, my heart began racing a million miles per hour.

No. Jamie Jackson *can not* be here in the gym right now, volunteering to help with decorating for the winter dance.

# Chapter Two

The hatred towards Jamie Jackson began way back when we were in kindergarten. He sat next to me in class and snatched the dark blue pencil I was using to color in my elephant on the coloring stencil. He didn't even ask if he could use it after I was finished with it. He just snatched it. I burst into tears right there, raising my hand and telling my teacher what he had done. Jamie only laughed and told me to suck it up, and that I shouldn't be a cry baby over a pencil.

Another time he asked me why was my hair red. I was the only redhead in my class. Sometimes he would tease me about it, saying how red hair wasn't even a color.

In third grade, our class was putting on Peter Pan. I wanted to play the part of Wendy Darling in the play. My third-grade teacher decided to cast Jamie as Peter Pan. Later, he said to me I couldn't be Wendy because she didn't have red hair. My teacher ended up casting me as a mermaid.

There was another time where he kicked a soccer ball at my

head. He said it was an accident, but we both know it wasn't. He was so damn lucky that I didn't get a concussion from it.

I could go on and on about what that jerk does to me. It's like he enjoys being my number one enemy. I will be glad once I can get out of Parkerville next fall and go to college. I will die if Jamie attends the same college as me. What are the odds he does?

"You have got to be kidding me," I say to Allegra. "What is he doing here?"

Allegra shrugs. "Volunteering like everyone else?"

Jamie catches my eye and smirks. He makes his way up the stairs, winks at me and continues to the back row. I look back at him as he sits down, his bag on the seat beside him. He had the whole back row to himself.

"Okay, can I have your attention please?" Miss Fields says.

We settle down. I try to focus on the teacher, but I could feel Jamie's eyes on the back of my head. I didn't dare to look back at him. I keep eyes focus on Miss Fields, waiting her to continue on.

"I want to thank you all for coming this afternoon," she continues. "I know it's the start of Christmas break, and you all want to get home as soon as possible, so I will make this brief. The dance committee and I have come up with a theme for next year's winter dance at the end of January. It's going to be a snowflake theme. Once we get back from the break, I will be assigning you tasks to prepare for the dance. Over the break you can think about what decorations we could use. Are there any questions?"

Someone raises their hand and Miss Fields points to them. I tune out, glancing over my shoulder at Jamie. He stares back at me, that stupid smirk still on his face. I turn back to the front and try my best to listen to the questions. After two more questions, Miss Fields dismisses us. I spring to my feet and hurry off the bleachers. I don't even wait for Gabriella and Allegra as I walk out of the gym as fast as I can. I wanted to get as far away from that jerk as fast as I could.

"Candice, wait up," Allegra calls out to me as I step out of the gym.

I stop in the corridor and turn around to face her. "Sorry. I just really want to get out of here before Jamie comes."

Stepping through the door, Jamie walks out with his bag strap over his shoulder. He strolls over to Allegra and me.

"I didn't expect to see you volunteering for the dance, O'Connor," he says, standing next to Allegra, his eyes on me.

"Yeah, well the same thing goes for you," I say, frowning. "What are you, captain of the ice hockey team, doing volunteering for the dance?"

"Is there a crime in me wanting to help out with the dance?"

"Yes. Everything you do is a crime."

He steps closer to me. "Gee, that's a shame because no one else in this school thinks it. Maybe you and I will get to work on a task together when we get back. Wouldn't that be fun?"

I narrow my eyes at him. How does he get away with saying all of this stuff to people? Why do people find it so charming that he does? "I'm not working with you."

"That's a shame, O'Connor. I'm sure we are going to have fun together." He looks over at Allegra then back at me. "Well, you ladies have a good holiday. See you after the break."

"The same thing goes for you, Jamie," Allegra says.

Jamie turns to me like he was expecting for me to say something. When I don't, he winks at me before walking down the corridor without another glance.

Oh gosh, I think I'm going to be sick.

"I swear I have never seen so much hate between someone besides you two," Allegra says. "I can't believe how much you've hated each other since kindergarten."

"Yeah, and I can't wait until we graduate and I'd never have to see that jerk again."

Gabriella steps out of the gym. "I'm ready to go."

I smile. "Great." I turn to Allegra. "Would you like a lift home?"

Allegra normally catches the bus to and from school. But since the bus has already left, to save her walking to the nearest bus stop, I might as well drive her home.

"That would be great, thanks Candice," Allegra says.

The three of us head out to the car park. I look around, hoping not to bump into Jamie. I see him across the parking lot, getting into his own vehicle. I unlock my car and climb into the driver's seat without another glance at him. Gabriella takes the front passenger seat while Allegra sits in the back behind my sister.

"I can't believe Jamie is volunteering to help with the dance," I say as I pull out of the parking lot.

"It surprised me too," Gabriella says. "He came up to me after lunch and asked if he could sign up. He then apologized to me for the way his friends acted when I approached them."

I raise my eyebrows, glancing at her before turning back to the road. "Jamie Jackson apologized? Wow, I didn't know he had the heart to apologize."

"Whatever happened between you two?" Gabriella wanted to know. "Why do you hate each other so much?"

Allegra scoffs in the backseat. "Don't get her started on

that, Gabriella. Jamie and Candice have been fighting since kindergarten."

"The jerk snatched the coloring pencil I had in my hand," I explain to my sister. "He didn't even ask me if he could use it. He just snatched it right out."

"And that, Gabriella, is the start of how Candice O'Connor and Jamie Jackson became enemies."

"Wow," Gabriella says. "Why don't you do a truce? I mean, if you guys are going to work on the decorations for the dance next month, then you might as well call it a truce. You can't be enemies forever."

I scoff. "I'm sure we can be enemies forever. And I doubt we will ever call a truce. Even if it just for the dance."

"Well, whatever is going on between you two, please don't cause problems when we start putting the decorations up. I'm very excited that Miss Fields has asked me to be in charge of decorations this year. I don't want to screw this up."

I slow to stop at an intersection. I turn to my sister, giving her an assuring smile. "Don't worry, Gabriella. Everything will be fine. The dance will be great, and I'm so happy that Miss Fields asked you to help out with it all."

My sister returns a smile. "Thanks, Candice."

I start driving again.

"Hey Candice, Christmas is in a few days, and it means not thinking about Jamie for two weeks," Allegra says. "Just relax and enjoy the holidays. You won't relax if you think about him."

I drew in a deep breath, and tell myself to do just that. Allegra is right. For two weeks there would be no Jamie Jackson. No school to worry about. Just a holiday to spend time with my family. It's going to be fun.

Although forgetting that jerk was easy said than done. He was *always* at the back of my mind, knowing exactly what he will say with a sarcastic comment. I can never forget anything he says to me. And for this winter holiday, I want to not have to think about him.

# Chapter Three

Okay, so the whole forgetting about Jamie Jackson didn't really last long. As soon as I got home, I sit on my bed and browse through Instagram. I couldn't search for him on Facebook, as I had to add him as a friend. But on Instagram I was able to view his profile without having to follow him. I scroll through his profile, staring at his life in photos, feeling disgusted as I do.

I stare at pictures of his friends and family. There was one photo where he posed with his golden retriever. His latest photo was posted not long ago, where he is standing in front of his car in the school's parking lot. He holds up a peace sign as he takes the selfie. Underneath his photo is the caption: *School's out.*

Why do I look at his social media profiles? I don't really know.

The door to my bedroom that I share with Gabriella, opens. Gabriella walks in with Hannah behind her. Hannah is carrying our cat Belle, who is a ragdoll.

"Can you believe it that we are finally going to Rocky Springs tomorrow?" Hannah literally bounces as she strolls over to me. She sits down on the bed, glancing at the screen on my phone. "Who is Jamie Jackson? Is he your boyfriend?"

I laugh hysterically. "That would be the day."

"Why are you looking up Jamie?" Gabriella asks as she leans against the ladder for our bunk beds. "I thought you hated him."

I put my phone down on the bed. "I do."

"Then why look him up? Unless of course you have a secret crush on him and you don't want anyone to know."

I pretend to vomit. "Please."

Gabriella stares at me for what feels like a long time before she shrugs. "If you say so."

"Why don't you like him?" Hannah asks me.

I roll my eyes. "Let's not worry about him, okay? Let's talk about the trip." I take Belle from my sister and put her on my lap, stroking her. Belle purrs as she relaxes.

"I'm so happy we are finally going to Rocky Springs!" Hannah leaps off of the bed, jumping up and down on the spot. "It has felt like the day would never get here."

She loves winter. Her favorite movie is *Frozen*, and every time it starts snowing, she goes around the house singing *Do You Want to Build A Snowman?* We have gone on a couple of weekend ski trips here in New York, and I swear she gets excited more than anyone in the house. I may have grown up with snow, but it's not something I enjoy very much. The snow is beautiful, but I hated shovelling the driveway.

"I know, it has totally felt like ages," Gabriella says.

Hannah reaches over to scratch behind Belle's ears. "I wish

we could take Belle with us. I think she would really like it."

"I'm sure Belle will enjoy her time with Grandma and Grandpa," I tell her. "We will only be gone for a week."

"I know." Hannah takes the cat from me, and holds Belle in the air. "And when I get back, Belle, we will play out in the snow together."

Belle replies with a meow. Hannah hugs her.

There's a knock on the door and Mom walks in.

"What are you girls up to?"

"Talking about the trip," I say.

"Have you finished packing everything you want to take?"

"I have!" Hannah says excitedly.

Gabriella nods. "I have too."

Everyone turns to me, waiting for me to answer. Okay, so maybe instead of finishing packing, I was stalking Jamie online. I mean, most of things are packed. I still have to pack my snow boots that are in my closet, and I'm trying to figure out where I had put my skiing googles.

"I'm almost finished packing," I answer.

"Okay, well dinner is ready," Mom announces. "So let's all come down to eat. And after dinner, Candice, I want you to finish packing. Hannah, Gabriella, later bring your suitcases down to the living room. Grandma and Grandpa will come by in the morning to pick us up for the airport."

I nod, picking up my phone from the bed, and then follow my sisters and Mom out of my room to the kitchen.

"I wish Grandma and Grandpa could come with us," Hannah says.

"I know, sweetie," Mom says. "I would love it too if my parents were to come along. The next vacation we go on we will definitely invite them."

"I can't wait for all of the Christmas activities we will be able to do there."

"It will be a magical experience."

Dad is serving up the food when we walk in. Hannah puts Belle down, and she runs off somewhere in the house while we sit down to eat dinner.

Later that night, when Gabriella and I settle into bed for the night, she says, "I think you like him, Candice."

I sit up, peeking over the edge of the bunk bed where my sister slept on the bottom. "Like who?"

"Jamie Jackson."

I snort. "I hate Jamie Jackson."

"That's what you say. But the way you two act around each other, like there's all of this tension between you two, even with all of the hatred, I think you secretly like him. I think he likes you too. Neither of you want to admit it, though."

"Where are you getting this, Gabriella? What makes you think I like him?"

"Well, for one, you stalk his social media pages and you also always talk about him. So I think you are curious about him, but you are denying your feelings."

Me, Candice Abigail O'Connor, secretly liking Jamie Jackson, the biggest jerk on this planet? Excuse me while I laugh.

There is no way was I ever going to like that guy. Even if he was the last guy on Earth.

"I don't like him, Gabriella," I say, lying back down on my bed. "I will never like him."

Gabriella doesn't answer straight away. "Okay. If you say so."

My sister leaves the conversation there, and drifts off to

sleep. I lay there for a moment, thinking, as I stared into the darkness. I wonder what had made my sister think that I was secretly crushing on the guy I hated the most. I couldn't even imagine myself falling for a guy who is so full of himself.

# Chapter Four

My sisters and I were seated together on the plane, while my parents sat two rows ahead of us. Dad helped us to get our luggage in the upper cabins before taking his seat with Mom. Hannah sat by the window, glancing out. Gabriella sat in the middle, and I had the aisle seat.

"Fancy seeing you here, O'Connor."

I snap my head in the voice's direction. Gabriella looks over as well. Sitting in the opposite aisle seat is none other than Jamie Jackson. He has a huge smirk on his face, and all I want to do was wipe it off him.

"What are you doing here, you jerk?" I frown. "Are you stalking me?"

Jamie laughs hysterically. "Stalking you? Oh, Candice, why would I be stalking you?"

"You are on the same flight as me. Why?"

Jamie shrugs. "I can't help it that my parents booked the same flight as yours."

"Please tell me you aren't going to the same place as us. Please tell me you are going to Los Angeles for the holidays." We have a layover in Los Angeles before boarding another flight to Colorado.

Jamie shakes his head. "Nope, I'm not heading to Los Angeles for Christmas."

"Then where are you heading?"

"Where are you heading?"

Gabriella sighs beside me. "Are you guys going to argue the whole flight?"

Jamie and I turn to her. "No."

"Good. Just kiss and make up already, okay? I would like to enjoy this flight without hearing you."

Jamie and I look at each other. It made me think of what she had said last night, about how I could secretly like him. The thought of it made me want to throw up. I look at Jamie with a disgusted look. Yeah, his lips may look kissable, but he was surely the last person on Earth I wanted to kiss.

I turn to Gabriella, who is glancing at something on her phone before she had to switch it to flight mode. "Can we swap seats?"

Gabriella shakes her head, looking up at me. "No. I don't like the aisle seat."

I sigh, resting my head against the head rest. Why am I on the same flight as this jerk? He is going to irritate me all through this flight. I just know he will.

This is not the start of the Christmas vacation I wanted.

\* \* \*

Once in the air, I do everything I can do to concentrate on

the book I had brought along. Hannah was busy coloring in her book and Gabriella was reading. But it didn't matter how much I try to concentrate on the words I was reading, but I couldn't. I haven't looked Jamie's way once, but I'm one hundred percent sure he has looked my way a few times. I can feel his brown eyes burning into me. It was a six hour flight to Los Angeles, and I didn't need that creep staring at me for that long.

Eventually, I couldn't concentrate on the book any longer and decided to take a walk. I tell my sisters I am going to go to the bathroom. I put my bookmark in between the pages of my book and get up, walking to the back of the plane. One of the bathrooms was unoccupied, and I enter it, locking the door behind me.

I rest my back up against the door in the cramped bathroom and sigh, rubbing my hands over my face. I still can't believe I'm on the same flight with Jamie Jackson. I was hoping I wouldn't have to worry about him for two weeks, but here I am with him. And why do I get the feeling that he isn't just going to Los Angeles? I don't think I could handle it if he too was going to spend his winter break in Rocky Springs. I really do not want to see him around the town for the week.

A knock on my door snaps me out of my thoughts.

"O'Connor?"

I frown. Seriously? This idiot is following me to the bathroom now? Why can't he leave me alone?

I unlock the door and open it a crack. There, standing outside the door, is Jamie. "What do you want?"

"Can I come in?"

I frown. "What? You can't use a different bathroom?"

"I don't want to use the bathroom. I want to talk to you."

I raise an eyebrow. "What? In here?"

He nods. "Yes, in there. Would you rather have the conversation out here?"

"It's not like anyone would care if we did."

"Only if you want them to be staring at us all through the flight."

"What do you want to talk about?"

"Us."

I roll my eyes. "Listen, I'm not interested in you and I do not want to talk about *us*."

"I don't mean it like that. Please, Candice? I promise I won't talk to you for the *rest* of the flight."

I look around the bathroom. Did he seriously wanted to come in this cramped bathroom just to talk?

I move aside and let him in. I lean against the sink while he leans up against the door. It's so cramped that there isn't even any space between us. The thought of us standing extremely closed terrifies me. What was he going to do to me in here? Didn't he torture me enough? There is nothing for us to talk about.

"So? What do you want to talk about?" I ask him.

"We should make a truce."

I raise an eyebrow. "You want to make a truce? Why?"

He shrugs. "I think it's about time we make one. Besides, we don't exactly want to murder each other on this flight, do we? So what do you say, O'Connor? I mean, your sister did say we should kiss and make up."

I look at him disgusted. "No. I am not kissing you."

"And I'm not kissing you either."

"Good." I point towards the door. "How about you get out of here then?"

He stares at me long and hard without moving. Did he not hear what I had said?

"So where are you spending your Christmas?" he asks.

I frown. "I thought I told you to get out."

"Hey, I'm just making conversation. Let's make a truce, and be friends. Friends make conversation, don't they?"

I burst into laughter at this. "Seriously? You want to be friends? Jamie, you and I can never be friends. You made it pretty clear since kindergarten that we will never be friends."

Jamie blinks a few times. "How did I make that clear?"

"By snatching the dark blue pencil I was using out of my hand so you could use it. You could have asked politely if you could use it after me, but you didn't."

Jamie laughs at this. "Oh my gosh. Seriously, Candice? You're mad about something stupid I did as a kid? Come on, we all do silly things like that when we were kids. I, for one, was a little brat."

"Well, I wasn't like you. I was taught to have manners."

"So was I."

I scoff. "It didn't seem like you did. I mean, that wasn't the only thing you did to me."

Jamie raises his eyebrow. "Damn. There must be a lot of things I have done to upset you. Should I go and ask the flight attendant for some popcorn? I will enjoy this story a lot more if I was eating popcorn."

I roll my eyes. "I don't need to list everything."

"Okay, well give me one thing then."

"You hate my hair."

"Since when did I ever say I hated your hair?"

"Everyday. You always ask me why my hair is red, only because I was the *only* redhead at school. And that time in third grade when I wanted to be Wendy Darling in our school play, you said Wendy doesn't have red hair. And just yesterday you asked if I was adopted all because my sister doesn't have my hair color."

Jamie shrugs, like what I had said was no big deal. "I was just curious about you being adopted. I didn't mean to offend you."

I cross my arms, which brushed up against his chest. "What did I ever do to you to make you such a jerk around me?"

Jamie points to himself. "Me?" He shakes his head. "Nothing. Maybe it's just you. You seem to be the one who gets annoyed being around me. I only add to your annoyance." He smirks.

I clench my jaw. Was it possible that I could throw him out of this plane? "Can I ask why you signed up to help with decorating for the winter dance?"

"I wasn't going to, and then I saw you signing up for it. So I approached your sister and told her I had changed my mind about signing up. I thought it might be fun to work alongside you."

I stare at him. "Seriously? You signed up to annoy me?"

Jamie shrugs. "Your words, not mine. I just thought that because I'm the captain of the hockey team maybe it would be good for me sign up for this. It will look good on my college applications."

"Yeah, I don't think helping with decorating the school dance is going to help with boosting your ego. It's not even going to help you to get into college."

"Who says it wouldn't?"

"Look, can you get out of here? I can't stand to look at you any longer, let alone talk to you."

"You know, you can't stay in here for the whole flight."

I place my hands on his chest, attempting to distance him from me, but the little space we have doesn't allow it. "Just get out."

Jamie opens the door. But before he steps out, he turns to me. "Oh, by the way. To answer your question, I'm going to Rocky Springs to spend Christmas with family at the ski resort."

I freeze, my eyes widening. He gives me one final smirk before stepping out of the bathroom.

Jamie Jackson is spending Christmas at the *exact* same resort as me.

You have got to be kidding me.

# Chapter Five

I'm one hundred percent sure Jamie set a curse upon me that day he snatched the pencil out of my hand. It's like he made himself to be my number one enemy in life and irritate me with everything he does. How we have ended up going to the same ski resort this year, I wasn't sure.

As soon as we get off the plane, waiting for our next flight to Rocky Springs, I call Allegra.

"You will never guess who is here," I say as soon as she answers the phone.

"I don't know. Who?"

"Jamie Jackson." His name slips off my tongue like it was poison.

Allegra is silent for a moment as she lets this sink in. "Are you serious?"

I nod. "Yup." I pop the p. "He is spending the break at Rocky Springs Ski Resort also. Can you believe it?"

"Wow. Well, when you get to the resort, concentrate on

spending time with your family, okay? Don't let him ruin your holiday."

*That's easy said than done*, I think.

"I will try. I will call you when I get to the resort."

"Have a safe flight, Candice."

I hang up, slipping the phone back into the pocket of my jeans. I started walking back to my family where they sat near the gate of our next flight, when I hear his voice.

"Talking about me, huh?" I spin around to face him. He stands there casually, like we were great pals, slipping his hands in the pockets of his jeans. "Do you talk about me often?"

I stare at him. "Are you stalking me?"

He shakes his head. "It's a bit hard to stalk someone when you are literally in the same building."

"Well, please stand somewhere else so I don't have to see you."

Jamie laughs. "That's going to be hard when we are basically spending the entire vacation in the same place. Come on, O'Connor. You know you love seeing my face."

I clench my fists at my side. "Can you stop calling me by my surname? I'm not one of your teammates. My name is Candice."

"Okay, Candice," he says with a smirk.

I roll my eyes, and turn to walk back to my family.

"You know you love me, O'Connor," he calls out to me. "Just admit it already."

I turn to face him, that ugly smirk on his face. "Never in a million years, *Jackson*."

I sit next to Gabriella, who still has her nose in a book. Hannah sat beside her, resting her head against Mom's shoulder. Dad sat next to her, looking at something on his phone. I glance at my own phone to check the time. There was still another twenty minutes before we board our second flight.

"Trouble in paradise with your boyfriend?" Gabriella asks me without looking up from her book.

I look at her. "Who said he was my boyfriend?"

She puts the bookmark in between the pages and closed it, turning to me. "You guys fight like a married couple."

"Yeah, right."

"You can keep denying it all you want, Candice, but I still think you like him."

"I don't like him."

Gabriella shrugs and went back to her book.

I glance over my shoulder to see if Jamie was still standing where I had left him. He wasn't. He was now sitting down in a row of chairs not far from us, sitting with a woman and man who looked to be his parents. They had the same dark brown hair as him. I hold my gaze on him for a second before he must have sense me watching him and looks my way. I quickly turn and sit there, pulling out my phone, which I stared at for the remainder of the twenty minutes before we started boarding the plane.

\* \* \*

The last seat on the shuttle bus to take us from the airport to the resort happened to be next to Jamie. I sit in the aisle seat without looking at him.

Why, oh, why is this happening to me? What did I ever do to have this guy torture me?

"Hey, it's nice seeing you again, stranger," Jamie says.

Keeping my eyes ahead, I say, "Please do not talk to me

for the rest of this bus ride. Better yet, stay away from me completely once we get to the resort."

"Aw, did someone wake up on the wrong side of the bed this morning? Is this why you don't seem so happy?"

I shoot him a look. "Seriously, Jamie? Do you have to be so sarcastic?"

He shrugs. "It's just the kind of person I am."

"Well, stop. I don't like you, and you don't like me. So why don't we just leave each other alone during this vacation?"

"I don't know how that's going to work, Candice."

"Well, we will make sure it works."

"So that truce I wanted to make on the plane isn't going to happen, is it?"

I scoff. What was the use of making a truce when it will never work between us? "No, it's never going to happen. We are two different people who hate each other's guts."

"Hate is such a strong word."

The bus began moving along.

"You know, I really don't know how we are not going to see each other on this trip," Jamie carries on. "We are going to be in the same resort, O'Connor. We are going to be seeing each other all the time."

I shoot him a look. Why hasn't he stopped talking to me yet? "Well, as soon as we get to the resort, just stay away from me, okay?"

His lips curl into a smirk and shrugs. "If you say so."

We stay silent for the rest of the trip, and I was thankful he hadn't talked to me the whole fifteen-minute drive to the resort.

As soon as the shuttle bus pulls up in front of the lodge, I scramble out of my seat before that jerk could follow me, grabbing my luggage from outside the bus while I waited for my parents and sisters. The five of us head inside the resort. Dad made his way over to the front desk to check us into our room. Mom stands with him, while my sisters and I stand around the tall Christmas tree in the lobby. Around the room is decorated nicely with garland and lights, and it looks spectacular with the rustic interior. We didn't put up our tree this year or any decorations at our house since we were spending the holidays here. Our family also agreed on no gifts this year, as this vacation was our gift. The Rocky Mountains has been on our bucket list for some quite time. We often did weekend getaways at the ski resorts back in New York, and it was nice to be able to go somewhere different.

"This tree is so amazing!" Hannah says, craning her neck to get a better look at the top.

The tree was lid up with colorful lights with silver and gold tinsel decorated around the tree with ornaments, and a gold star right on top of the tree,

"It is," Gabriella says.

I look behind me, in time to see Jamie walking inside with his parents, their luggage rolling in behind them. He hasn't seen me yet.

"Have you messaged Edward to let him know we are here?" Mrs. Jackson asks her husband.

Mr. Jackson nods. "Yes. He said he will meet us after his shift ends at five."

Mrs. Jackson looks around the lobby, then points at something that is past the tree. "Oh look, there's Estelle and Francois."

And that's when Jamie looks my way. Our eyes meet and I quickly turn back to the tree.

*Pretend he isn't here*, I tell myself.

I was glad when my parents came to our side, telling us where we are going. Without looking back at Jamie, I follow my family up to our room on the second floor.

Like the lobby, the room also had a rustic interior as we were staying inside a cabin with the wooden walls. As we enter the room, we had the bathroom to our right. Across from that bathroom is a bedroom with a bunk bed and twin bed. Next to the bathroom is another bedroom with a Queen bed. Past the bedrooms is an open space with a living room. There's a fireplace with a TV above it. On the other side of the room is the dining area with a small kitchen. It felt so homey and cosy. There's also a balcony that looks out over the pool and a spectacular mountain view beyond it. The ski slopes were a five-minute walk from the lodge.

"This place is awesome!" Hannah says. She drops her suitcase in the middle of the hallway, runs over to the couch, and jumps onto it.

"Hannah, don't jump on the furniture," Mom warns her in a firm voice.

"The mountain view is breathtaking," I point out.

Dad nods. "It sure is. Okay, ladies. Let's put our luggage away. Then we can relax before we head for dinner. How does that sound?"

We all agreed to Dad's suggestion. My sisters and I enter our bedroom. Hannah squeezes her way through Gabriella and I, dumping her suitcase in the middle of the floor, and then began climbing the ladder of the bunk bed.

"I get the top bunk!" she cries out.

Gabriella sits down on the bottom bunk, leaving me to sit on the twin bed.

"What should we do tomorrow?" Hannah asks, peeking over the railing. "Should we build a snowman?"

"I'm sure we are going to have plenty of time to build a snowman, Hannah," I tell her. "I'm sure Mom and Dad will want to go grocery shopping so we aren't always eating out. I plan to go snowboarding."

"I might give skiing a go this time instead of snowboarding," Gabriella says.

"I don't know what I'm going to do yet," Hannah says.

"You will figure it out," I say. "Maybe you can try a new skill."

"Maybe."

I get off the bed. "I'm going to check out the view on the balcony."

"I'm going to come too!" Hannah started making her way down the ladder.

Gabriella follows us out onto the balcony. I shiver briefly from the cold, and stand at the railing. There were a few people swimming. The sun was starting to set, turning the sky a shade of pink and purple over the mountains.

"Fancy seeing you here, O'Connor. Looks like we are going to be neighbors during this vacation."

My head snaps to the left. Standing on the balcony next door to us is none other than Jamie Jackson, a smirk is plastered on his lips.

Oh, come on! Seriously? What did I do to have this jerk stalk me all winter break?

Without a word, I headed inside. Can this vacation get any worse?

# Chapter Six

If I scream loud enough, would it be enough for an avalanche to come crashing down the mountain and sweep Jamie far away from me? Have him buried deep under the snow?

How can the one person I hate more than anything in this world be at the exact same resort as me? It just didn't seem possible for both of us to be here at the same time. It's bad enough we live in the same suburb and go to the same high school. I really am starting to think that Jamie somehow cursed me from all those years ago. It's the only explanation for why he keeps showing up everywhere. Otherwise, we wouldn't have gotten onto the exact same plane to this resort and rooms right next to each other. What else is going to happen on this trip? Do I even want to know?

Thankfully, when my family went out for dinner later that night, Jamie was nowhere to be seen. It was great to finally be alone with my family without having him around to ruin it all for me. As we waited for our food, my parents told us that after breakfast tomorrow we would be taking a trip to the grocery store to stock up on some food, in case we decided to eat in or to have some snacks. It was something my parents wanted to do before we go out on the slopes. It was fine by me as long as I didn't see Jamie.

After dinner we headed back to the room, deciding to get an early night after the long trip we had made today. As soon as my head hit the pillow, I was fast asleep.

The next morning, we head down to the dining room at the lodge, where a buffet breakfast is served. The smell of the food fills the air as soon as we walked in, my stomach grumbling. Hannah was the first to reach the table, making a bee line towards the pancakes. She stacks four on her plate before drowning them with maple syrup, making her way to a dining table near the buffet and digging into the pancakes.

I survey the buffet, trying to decide what I wanted for breakfast. There was a variety of scramble eggs, bacon, sausages, toast, pancakes and waffles, as well as many other foods that made my mouth water. I reach for two waffles, but instead of drowning it with maple syrup like my baby sister would have, I pour chocolate sauce over it, with some fruit salad to the side. I also grabbed a slice of toast and some scrambled eggs.

I'm about to turn from the buffet to head back to my table when the voice I never want to hear again started talking.

"Good morning, O'Connor. Did you sleep well?"

I turn to Jamie, a plate in his hand. He already scooped two sausages, bacon, and eggs onto his plate.

"Are you going to stalk me all vacation?" I ask him.

He looks at me. "Hey, that's not how you say good morning back."

I roll my eyes. "So?"

"So, you are supposed to say 'Good morning to you too, Jamie. Why yes, I did sleep well.' And for your information, I'm not stalking you." His lips curl into a smirk.

"Whatever. Just stay away from me."

Jamie shrugs, grabbing a slice of toast from the table. "I will try, but I can't guarantee that I will."

I walk away from him and sit down next to Hannah. Gabriella came back with a glass of orange juice.

"Who were you talking to, Candice?" Mom asks me with a smile. "Did you make friends already?"

I scoff as I cut a piece of my waffle. "Friends is not what I would describe us."

"It happens to be her boyfriend, who she won't admit she likes," Gabriella speaks up.

I look at my sister, my fork mid-way to my mouth with a piece of waffle and a cut up strawberry on top. My sister seriously did not just say that. "I do not like the jerk."

Gabriella makes eye contact with me. "Well, you talk about him enough. Just admit it already that you like him."

"Wait, am I missing something?" Dad asks, putting down his fork. He looks directly at me. "Are you seeing someone without your mother and I knowing?"

"Relax, Dad," I assure him. "I'm not dating anyone. And Jamie Jackson is *not* someone I would like to date. He is so full of himself." I place the waffle in my mouth.

Mom looks over in the direction of Jamie before turning back to me. "Jamie Jackson, the captain of the ice hockey team at your school?"

"Yes."

"Well, isn't it interesting that he is staying at the same lodge as us."

I almost spill the jug of water on the table when I went to pour myself a glass.

"Yes, it is interesting that he is here," I answer. I take a sip of my drink.

"I hope you get to find some time to hang out with him while we are here. Maybe you two will become friends if you aren't already."

Over my dead body would I ever want to spend time hanging out with him.

Instead of arguing about that jerk, I dug into my breakfast. I wasn't going to ruin my appetite over him. As I ate, my parents talked about how we were going to spend our day. I was glad that Gabriella and I were allowed to go off onto the slopes on our own, but Hannah had to be with either one of us or our parents. I couldn't wait to hit the slopes once we get back from shopping.

As we get up to leave to head out, I glance over at the Jackson family. Jamie is sitting at the table with his parents. There was also some guy and lady sitting with them who I didn't recognize. It was like he could sense me looking, and turns in my direction. Our eyes meet, and I swiftly turn before we could have a staring competition, one that I did not want to have.

* * *

"Why did you tell Mom and Dad that Jamie Jackson is my boyfriend?" I ask Gabriella as we walk out of a café, where we had gotten ourselves a hot chocolate. She also carried one for Hannah, who was with our parents in the grocery store. "You know he isn't."

Gabriella sighs. "Candice, we have been over this so many times. It's obvious that you do like him. You just won't admit it."

"There's nothing for me to admit."

"Look, do we really need to have this conversation again?"

That I couldn't guarantee because I'm always going to bring up Jamie in a conversation, and about everything that irritates me about him.

"We can stop having this conversation if you promise me you aren't going to call him my boyfriend," I say. "Especially to Mom and Dad."

Gabriella nods, taking a sip of her drink. "Okay. I won't say anything, and I will keep my comments to myself, even if I do think you're secretly crushing on him but don't even know it yourself."

I chuckle at this. "Yeah, I'm pretty sure I'm not crushing on him. He will be the last person I would ever crush on."

We leave the conversation as that, because the last thing I wanted was to get into a fight with my sister. I don't like fighting with my sisters, and I mostly didn't want to ruin this vacation for either of us all because of some stupid argument about a boy who I hate. Jamie Jackson is not worth getting into fights about.

We find our parents in the grocery store, and Gabriella hands Hannah her hot chocolate. We had offered to get our parents something, but they didn't want anything.

As I walk alongside my family, grabbing things for our holiday, I pull out my phone and decided to scroll Instagram. Making sure Gabriella wasn't looking my way, I click on Jamie's profile to see if he had updated anything. He had uploaded a new photo. He is standing out on the balcony of his room, the pool and the snow-capped mountains behind him. His caption reads: *Looking forward to this winter getaway.* Next to his caption was a skier emoji.

I stare at the photo for a long time as we walk, wondering why my sister would think I had a crush on this guy. Sure, Jamie is cute and has these gorgeous brown eyes and an amazing smile, but he just wasn't my type.

I get out of his profile before Gabriella glances my way and sees what I'm looking at. I scroll down the page, liking several pictures from classmates or celebrities I follow. Allegra posted a selfie of her in front of her lit up Christmas tree with the caption: *Two days to go* with Christmas tree, present, and Santa emojis.

I close out of Instagram and put my phone away. We are heading to the check-out line, and the excitement builds for being able to hit the slopes after this shopping trip.

Let's hope I don't come across that jerk while I'm up there.

# Chapter Seven

My family and I go our separate ways once we get to the ski slopes. Gabriella went to learn how to ski like she had said she wanted to do, and my parents went with Hannah, who wanted to go snow tubing. I make a note to myself to give snow tubing a go later today. But right now, I was on my own, and I want to go snowboarding. Later, I will meet my family for lunch.

I stand in line for a chair lift. There is a couple of people in front of me.

The guy in front of me, who I recognize was sitting with Jamie's family this morning for breakfast, turns around, looking at something behind me. As soon as he looks my way, my heart jumps in my chest with how handsome this guy looks.

"Where is Jamie?" he says with a French accent. "He said he was coming up on the chairs with us, but he is nowhere to be seen."

I wanted to frown at the mention of the jerk's name, but

it was hard to frown when this handsome French man with an accent that sends my insides melting was standing right in front of me.

The lady standing next to him puts a hand on his shoulder. "He's coming, don't worry."

The couple in front of them got onto a chair. The lady turns around to face me. I recognize her as Estelle Jackson. Jamie's sister. She had lovely brown eyes and I could see some of the facial features she shared with Jamie. I knew Jamie had an older sister, but I have never met her. I have seen her at some of Jamie's games. Rumor has it that she was one of the top cheerleaders when she used to attend Parkerville High. I was thankful that these two were standing in front of me and not that idiot Jamie because there is no way would I even think about getting up on the same mountain as him. Hopefully I'm able to get down the mountain before he comes up.

Estelle smiles at me. "Hey, sweetie. Why don't you go ahead of us?"

"Are you sure?" I ask, not wanting to feel like I was waiting impatiently. But if Jamie was going to join them, then I wanted to make sure I get up the mountain before them.

Estelle nods. "Yes, go ahead. We are just waiting for someone."

"Thanks." I smile at her and the French man.

I walk around them and sit down on the chair just as I hear the French man say, "Jamie, there you are. We thought you weren't coming."

I turn in the chair just in time to see Jamie approach the couple.

"Who says I wasn't coming?" Jamie says. Our eyes meet.

I turn to face forward as the chair moves me away from

them. I wait for a few minutes before looking back at him and see the three of them getting onto a chair behind me. For the rest of the ride up, I keep my eyes ahead to avoid meeting them with Jamie's.

Once up on top, I move away from the chair lift. Taking a good look around at my surroundings, and strap my other foot in. As I pull down my goggles, ready to surf down the mountain, someone approaches me.

"*Bonjour jolie demoiselle,*" the voice says.

I turn around, thinking that it was maybe the French man from the chair lift. But no. It wasn't even someone who was French. It was none other than Jamie Jackson.

He is smirking. He must have seen me drooling over that guy and thought he could come over here and use the language.

"Did you just speak French?" I ask, double checking to make sure that I wasn't hearing things.

"Yes, I did. I said 'Hello, beautiful lady.'"

"Why did you speak French?"

"Well, I saw you talking to my sister and brother-in-law when I walked over, and I saw how you were looking at Francois. You looked like you might faint."

I was thankful it was cold out and that Jamie wouldn't be able to tell if I am blushing or not. The redness is from the cold, right? There is no way I was letting him know that I secretly have a sweet spot for French guys. I find them very handsome, and just the thought of them speaking the language melts my insides. There was something about the language. After all, it is known as the language of love. I couldn't speak it, and wished I could, but I was thankful I wasn't learning it at school because then I would have Jamie in my class.

Without admitting that yes, I was crushing on his brother-in-law, I ask, "So what? You think you can speak the language of love with me?"

He shrugs. "I wanted to see how you would react if I spoke it."

"Is this how you pick up girls? By speaking to them in French, hoping they would be impressed, and then be swept off their feet and fall magically in love with you?"

Jamie holds up a hand. "Whoa, whoa, whoa. What kind of guy do you think I am?"

I think for a moment. "Exactly the kind of guy who would use the language of love to make girls go out with you. You aren't even French."

"No, I'm not French, but who says I can't speak it? And even if I wanted to impressed some girl with my language skills, why would I want to impress you with it?"

I shrug. "I don't know. You tell me. You are the one who has all of the girls swooning all over you back at school."

"I can't help it that I'm hot and sexy."

I roll my eyes. Here we go again with him thinking he is so irresistible to girls.

"Come on, O'Connor. I know you think I'm hot too. Admit it."

Jamie Jackson may be hot, but he wasn't the kind of guy I wanted to like. He was too full of himself for me. I'd rather choke on my own vomit than fall to my knees at his feet.

"What kind of girl do you think I am?"

Jamie stares at me, like he was searching for something in my face, anything to say that I could be lying to him. I mean, just because he is the captain of the ice hockey team back at school, doesn't mean I find him irresistible.

"Okay, so just because I decide to speak French, it doesn't mean I'm picking you up," Jamie tells me. "One, I study French at school."

"I know. Allegra is in your class."

He nods. "Right, she is. And two, I had to study French because my sister got married to Francois last summer… in France. And no, I have never picked up a girl using the language, not even while I was in France."

"Well, good because I'm not going to be the first girl you pick up."

"But if Francois spoke it, you would be swooning."

He wasn't wrong about that, but I wasn't about to admit it.

"So what if I did?"

"Say if I was French, would I then be attractive to you?"

"I wouldn't date you even if you were French."

"*Non?*" Jamie then speaks with a French accent. "What if you had met my French twin brother, you still wouldn't fall for me?"

I stare at him.

"Jamie, are you coming with us?" his sister calls out to him.

Jamie turns to her. "I will meet you down the hill. I'm just talking with my friend here."

Estelle gives us a smile before she and Francois ski down the slope.

Jamie turns back to me.

"Like I said, even if you were French, I still wouldn't like you. Not even if you had a French twin brother, because I'm sure he would be exactly like you. You, Jamie Jackson, I will never like. I hate you so much that I could just rip out my own eyes so I don't have to look at you."

He steps closer to me. "Well, Candice O'Connor, I hate you

too."

It may be freezing, but as Jamie steps closer to me, only leaving a small gap between us, I could feel his body heat bouncing off him. He steps so close to me that at first, I thought he might kiss me. The thought of his lips on mine sends my heart racing.

"But we shouldn't hate each other because hate is a strong word," he tells me.

"Yeah, well you made it pretty clear in kindergarten when you snatched the pencil right out of my hand that you didn't like me."

Jamie chuckles. "I can't believe you are still holding a grudge over something that happened when we were kids."

*And whose fault is that?* I wanted to say. He could have apologized for what he did, but no, he continued to find ways to irritate me or made fun of me, like his bad manners weren't his fault.

"Whatever."

"But I'm pretty sure underneath all of that hatred, you do have a soft spot for me." He smirks.

I frown. He is really asking for trouble. "I will never have a soft spot for you."

He steps backwards and I'm glad he did because I don't know how much I could handle with him standing so close to me.

"Let's make a bet, O'Connor."

I raise an eyebrow. "What kind of bet?"

"Let's race down this slope. If you win, you have to buy me a hot chocolate. But if I win, you have to kiss me."

I stare at him, my mouth slightly open. Seriously? He wanted me to kiss him? Just a few minutes a go he was saying he hated me too, and now he wanted me to kiss him. What was he trying to prove?

"You're kidding, right? About me kissing you if you won?"

"Come on, O'Connor. I know you want to kiss me. You love me. Just admit it."

I frown at him. "Never in a million years would I ever kiss you."

I turn from him.

"So, do we have a bet, O'Connor?" he asks me one last time.

He holds out his hand. I stare at it.

"I will only agree to the bet if I don't kiss you. I am *not* going to kiss you. Ever. How about you buy me that hot chocolate?"

Jamie thinks about this for a second and then nods. "Okay, O'Connor. You have a deal."

I shake his outstretched hand, both of us eyeing each other. He pulls down his goggles and straps in his foot.

"Ready... set... go!" Jamie cries out.

I set off down the slope, gliding past other skiers and snowboarders. I keep my eyes ahead, not even daring to look behind me to see where that jerk is. I can see the bottom of the slope, and I smile to myself as I knew I was so going to win this bet.

But before I could even think about claiming victory, Jamie zooms past me, spraying snow.

"Hey, watch it!" I yell.

"Sorry, O'Connor," he yells back.

I pick up speed to catch him. There was no way I was going to let him win. We are almost at the end of the slope when I reach him. I reach for the sleeve of his jacket. He moves slightly away.

"Don't even think about it, O'Connor."

"Think about what?"

"You aren't going to win."

"Oh yes, I am."

I go to push him, but instead he grabs my arm. He skids to a stop as we near the end. Caught off guard of him putting on the brakes, I forget my own. I lose my balance and tumble into the snow. With Jamie's hand still on me, he falls with me. He lands on top of me in the snow.

"Well, looks like it's a tie," he grins, making no effort to get his body off me.

"And what's the prize if it's a tie?"

He doesn't answer me straight away, just stares at me.

"How about that kiss?" he says with a smirk.

I push him off and he sits beside me. I push my goggles to the top of my head. "You are unbelievable."

I shake my head and unstrap my boots from the board.

"One kiss won't be so bad," he says.

I get off the snow and look down at him. "I hate you, Jamie. Okay? Find some other girl to speak French to and kiss her."

Without another word, I storm off.

# Chapter Eight

I don't mention about what happened between Jamie and me when I sit down to lunch with my family. I can imagine what Gabriella will say. Hannah may be nine, but I don't think she will quite understand anything, though she will ask me all sorts of questions I didn't want to answer. And then there's my parents who would want to know what is really going on between me and him, and I couldn't answer their questions either. I was afraid of answering Dad's questions the most. He has pretty much made the rule that my sisters and I couldn't date until we were eighteen. But I'm sure even when I turn eighteen in August next year, Dad still wouldn't like me dating someone. Whatever questions or concerns he has about Jamie, it doesn't matter because he will never have to worry about me dating him.

As we eat and talk about our morning, I couldn't help but think about what happened between Jamie and me out on the slope. I wonder if he was serious about wanting to kiss me, but

I'm sure that was him trying to be impressive like he is with the other girls back home. I know he and Chelsea Chamberlain had dated for a while.

For the rest of the afternoon I wanted to do my best to forget about him and spend time with my family. While Mom and Dad visited the spa to get massages, my sisters and I went out to the pool. It wasn't something I wanted to spend my afternoon doing, but Hannah wanted to go swimming. The pool was heated, and it was so warm that I didn't even want to get out. And even though I told myself to forget about him, I couldn't help but glance up in the direction towards his window while we were in the pool, wondering if there was a chance he would come to the balcony and see us. I hope he doesn't.

Later that evening, we went to a restaurant nearby the lodge for dinner. When we headed back, my parents suggested we head to the entertainment room at the lodge where they were doing Christmas karaoke. We sit down at a table, listening and cheering people as they sang. Dad orders eggnog for himself and Mom, while getting my sisters and I a hot chocolate.

Hannah gets up to sing a song. Gabriella is shy when it comes to performing, so I convince her to come up and sing with me. She protests at first, but then decided to get up there for the fun of it. Even Mom and Dad got up to sing. None of us were great singers, but we had fun anyway.

With the good time we have been having, I hadn't thought about Jamie since. Not until he suddenly appeared on the stage. I frown when I see him. How long had he been in this room, and why did I not notice him around before when I was up on the stage with my sister?

He spots me in the audience and smirks at me as he sings.

I will admit he was pretty good. I have never heard him sing before. I tear my eyes away from him. I'm not going to watch him perform, and maybe then he won't stare at me either.

The inside of my mug is now empty. I look up at my parents, raising my voice at them so they could hear me over the music. "Can I get another hot chocolate?"

Dad nods, taking out his wallet and hands me a ten dollar bill. "Of course you can get yourself one."

I take the money. "Thanks, Dad."

I get up and walk over to the bar, ordering my hot chocolate. I wait for a few minutes as it gets made, keeping my back to the stage. Jamie soon finishes up his song, and I was glad because I couldn't stand to hear him for another minute.

The server behind the bar hands me my hot chocolate. I thank him.

"I thought I was supposed to buy you a hot chocolate?"

I frown at the sound of his voice. I turn around and see Jamie standing behind me. "After the incident you pulled on me today, I don't need you to buy me one."

I go to move around him, but he stops me.

"Can I talk to you? Please, Candice?" he asks.

"No. I don't want to talk to you. Ever. I don't even want to see you for the rest of this trip."

"Please, Candice?" His eyes pleaded with mine to hear him out, and I wonder if this was about what happened earlier today. "Look, I know you hate me, but I really need to talk to you. Do you think we can step outside for a bit?"

I look down at the steaming hot chocolate in my hands then over at my family who are watching the next people on the stage. I can easily walk over there with my mug and sit down, forgetting all about what Jamie wants to say to me. But I decided to hear what he had to say. I don't want to, but maybe he would apologize for his actions earlier today. I really didn't want to hear his apology because I'm sure it will be all a joke, but I decided it was the right thing to do to hear him out.

"Okay. Let me put this down and tell my parents where I am going."

He nods. I stroll over to the table, and set my mug down.

"Mom, Dad, I'm just going to step outside for a bit," I say. I don't tell them I'm stepping outside with Jamie. I don't want them to start asking questions, and the last thing I wanted was for Dad to give me the Talk. Like, I haven't heard it a million times and we have talked about safe sex in health class. But honestly, they didn't need to worry about me. Jamie Jackson is the last person I would ever sleep with.

"Everything okay, sweetie?" Mom asks me.

I nod. "Yeah, I just need some air. I will be right back."

Gabriella looks my way, and I see her looking over my shoulder. Then she makes eye contact with me, and she knows I'm sneaking outside with Jamie. Later she is going to ask me about him, and all I'm going to hear from her is how I'm in denial. She can be convinced that there is something going on between Jamie and me all she wants, but she will soon see we are enemies who can never like each other.

I make my way back to Jamie, and together we walk outside. We stand aside from the entry so we aren't in anyone's way.

I cross my arms across my chest. "So what do you want to talk about?"

Jamie slips his hands into his jacket's pockets. "I just want to apologize for how I acted today. I shouldn't have tried to get you to kiss me. Although, I was joking with you. I didn't think you would be offended by what I had said."

I stare at him. I couldn't believe that Jamie was actually standing here in front of me, apologizing to me for something. It's the first time he has ever done this.

"What are you up to, Jamie?" I ask him straight out.

He takes his hands out of his pockets. "What makes you think I'm up to something?"

"Because you, Jamie Jackson, are always up to something. You would do anything to irritate me. I mean, you never apologize for upsetting me."

"Maybe I just want to do something different."

I laugh. "Yeah, I find that hard to believe."

"Look, I realize the way I acted today was something I shouldn't have done. I'm sorry, Candice."

I still wasn't sure if I could trust him. How do I know that as soon as I walk back inside that he wasn't going to do something behind my back?

I shiver briefly and glance back inside where it's nice and warm. I wanted to leave him out here, not accepting his apology because I really didn't think he was serious about being sorry. He is going to go right back to being a total jerk.

I then look in the direction of the snow and get an idea.

I walk down the stairs and scoop up some snow.

"Candice?" he calls out to me. "Are you going to accept my apology?"

I shrug. "That depends."

"On what?"

"How this snowball fight goes."

I turn to face him and threw the ball at him. It hits his chest. He smirks and bends down to pick up some snow. He then throws it at me. I dodge out of the way.

I stick out my tongue. "Missed me."

Jamie curls his lips into a smirk. "I will get you, O'Connor."

We grab more snow and hurl it at each other. He manages to dodge out of the way, my snowball flying past his shoulder. But I wasn't fast enough as his snowball hits me in the chest. I squeal as it does.

He throws his arm in the air as he scored victory. "Yes, victory!" He pulls his arm down, giving me a sneaky smile. "Told you I will get you, O'Connor."

"Maybe this time you did, but next time you won't."

"Do you want to bet?"

I scoop up some snow, and he does the same thing. We throw them at the same time, but the balls hit neither of us. They hit each other in the mid-air, exploding. Jamie and I burst into laughter.

"Catch me if you can, Jamie."

I take off, trying to run the best I can in the snow. I hear him crunching through the snow after me. I don't know how he catches me, but arms wrap around my waist, and he pulls me to the ground with him. He is laughing his head off. I remove his arms from around my waist and turn to him, shoving him hard.

"What on earth did you do that for?" I demand as I sit up.

He looks at me, innocent. "What? You said to catch you if I could."

I frown. "I didn't mean you could tackle me to the ground. I meant try and throw another snowball at me."

"No need to throw a hissy fit, O'Connor. I'm just having some fun."

"Well, I don't want to have fun with you. Find someone else to tackle in the snow."

I go to get up, but Jamie grabs my wrist.

"Hey, where are you going?"

I roll my eyes and turn to him. "Where does it look like I'm going? I'm going back inside to get away from you."

"Stay a little longer out here."

"And why would I want to stay out here with you?"

He shrugs. "I don't know. Maybe because I'm hot and sexy."

I shake my head. "You are so unbelievable. You are not hot and sexy."

Okay, so he was hot, but I was not going to let him think that I like him. He was no way near my type, no matter how sexy he may be. He was full of himself, and that I could not stand about him.

"You're lying to yourself," he says with a grin.

I scoff. "I'm not lying." I shake his hand off me.

"You definitely find my brother-in-law hot."

I blush at this. I was thankful that it was cold out and that my cheeks would have turned red from that. There is no way I wanted Jamie to see me blush. It's bad enough he teased me out on the mountain today for crushing on his brother-in-law, and then thought it was alright to try and pick me up by speaking French. I might have a soft spot for French guys, but I didn't appreciate Jamie speaking the language. It wasn't going to make me like him.

Instead of answering him, I go to get up. "I'm going to head back inside."

Jamie scramble to his feet. "What's the hurry, O'Connor?"

"I just want to head back inside to be with my family and where it's warm. And how many times do I need to tell you to call me by my first name, not my surname?"

Jamie shrugs. "I like calling you by your surname."

"Okay, well, I'm going to head inside now. I want to enjoy the rest of the night and hope the hot chocolate I bought has not gone cold."

As I turn once more, he grabs my wrist. I spin around, my hair whipping across my face. I frown at him.

"What is your problem?" I snatch my wrist out of his grip. "Why do you keep grabbing me?"

"Hang out with me for a little while longer."

Did he seriously wanted me to hang out with him a little while longer? Is he forgetting that we are enemies? We do not hang out together as enemies, let alone talk.

"Aren't you forgetting something, Jamie?" I ask him.

"Like what?"

I gesture between us. "Like how you and I are enemies. We don't hang out."

Jamie shrugs, not seeming to care what I had said. "So?"

I stare at him, trying to read him into seeing if he was up to something. He pretty much had a poker face, and I couldn't see if he was playing me or not. He has to be playing with me. He is no doubt up to something, and I wasn't going to fall for his tricks.

"Whatever you are up to, I don't want to be apart of it," I tell him.

"I'm not up to anything. I just want to hang out."

"So why hang out with me? You are here with your family, aren't you? Go and hang out with them. Hang out with anyone but me."

He stares at me for what seems like a long time, and it gives me goosebumps just thinking about his eyes on me. I look behind my shoulder towards the lodge behind me, hearing the laughter and Christmas music inside. If I make a run for it, will I be able to make it back inside without Jamie trying to catch me?

"This vacation was about hanging out with my family," Jamie tells me. "My brother had decided to stay here in Colorado after he graduated college not long ago, and had gotten a job at this resort. I haven't seen my sister since she got married last summer. This is the first time we are all together. Only now this vacation has turned into being about Francois and Estelle. After she went skiing today, she wasn't feeling well. And it turns out she hasn't been feeling well for the past week. She decided to take a pregnancy test today and found out she is expecting her first child. Everything is about her right now, and since I have gotten here, not once have my siblings asked me about how high school is going, what colleges I have in mind or how I'm doing in hockey."

There's silence between us as I let this sink in. At school, Jamie always seemed like this perfect jock that everyone looks up to. Ice hockey wasn't the only sport he played. He was one of the star athletes at our school who took part in one sport each season. In the fall he played football, ice hockey during the winter, and lacrosse during the spring. But then hearing him say all this, how he wasn't getting the attention he wanted really surprised me. Or maybe I shouldn't be surprised because at school many people worshipped him. That attention should be good enough for him, right?

"Have you decided on any colleges yet?" I ask him.

"I'm deciding between Boston University, Harvard, and Yale. I haven't decided exactly where I would like to go or what I would like to study. I'm hoping to score a scholarship to one of them." He slips his hands in his pockets. "I wouldn't mind playing for NHL though, but not sure if it's something I would be good enough for."

"Don't doubt yourself, Jamie. You never really know what can happen."

Oh my gosh, I can't believe I'm giving this guy advice. What is wrong with me?

Jamie nods slowly. "Yeah."

We sit there in silence for a second, unsure what to say to each other. Can we just end this conversation so I can go back inside?

"What about you?" Jamie breaks the silence. "Have you applied to any colleges yet?"

I shake my head. It's something I should be doing, but I haven't really decided on where I would like to go. "I'm looking into some colleges."

"Any idea where you would like to go?"

I shake my head. "No, not yet."

"You will find something soon."

He's right, but this isn't something I want to discuss with him.

"Look," I move on, "try not to worry so much about your family. Christmas is in two days, and you will be enjoying yourselves."

"I hope so."

We sit there in silence again. Okay, that's it. I really need to go inside. I have been out here long enough with him. I'm cold and all I wanted was to go back inside where it's warm, and to also be miles away from this jerk. He can find some other girl to hang out with.

"Well, if that's all, I'm going to head inside," I say.

"Do you want to go and hang out by the pool for a bit?" Jamie asks before I could turn and head back inside. "Not to go swimming, but to sit by it."

I sigh with frustration. Why does this guy want me around him tonight? Why can't he just let me go back inside and spend the night with my family? Why is it so hard for him to do that?

"Fine," I groan. "I will stay with you just for a little while and then I'm going to head back inside."

"Sweet," he says with a smile.

I roll my eyes at him. Can I wipe the smile off his face?

Jamie and I walk in silence towards the pool. In my mind, I plot out a way to ditch Jamie and head back inside with my family. I'm sure if I make a run for it I could, only the snow makes it impossible to run. And I'm sure that if I do make a run for it, being the athletic person he is, he will probably be able to reach me in no time, making sure I wasn't going anywhere. Out of all of the ski resorts in this country, why did Jamie's family choose this ski resort? Why did his brother work here? I could be having a wonderful vacation without him, but instead I'm spending it with him nearby.

No one is near the pool, so we pretty much have it to ourselves. I was glad because I didn't want anyone to see us together. Hopefully no one peeks out their windows and sees us. I don't want people to think 'Oh what a lovely couple they are', because honestly the thought of people thinking that made me sick. Jamie and I could never be a lovely couple even if we tried. We would fight like cats and dogs.

"You know, I think we are the only crazy ones out here near the pool right now," I point out to him.

Jamie nods. "We sure are."

I was about to sit down on a lawn chair when Jamie stops me.

"No, no." He points towards the water. "Let's sit on the edge of the pool."

Sitting beside the water seemed nice. Maybe dipping my feet into the heated water will help me to feel warm.

I'm about to sit down on the edge when Jamie says, "Do you have your phone on you?"

I look at him strangely, wondering why he would ask me for my phone. "Yes, of course I have."

"Can I see it before we sit down? I'm planning to get a new phone soon and I just want to see what kind you have."

I shrug, taking my phone out of my pocket and hand it to him. "My phone isn't exactly new, you know. It's like a year old."

Jamie takes my phone. "That's okay. I just want to see it."

I watch him carefully as he looks at my phone. When he looks up at me, I thought he was going to hand it back to me. Instead, he shoves his other hand at my chest and pushes me into the pool.

I barely have the time to register what had happened. I can't believe what that jerk did. I knew he was up to something. I should have left him outside and gone back to my family. But no, I had to keep him company. Only he had tricked me!

I resurface, spitting out chlorine water, and pushing my hair out of my face.

"Did you have a nice swim, O'Connor?"

I frown at him. "You jerk! Why did you do that for?"

Jamie shrugs. "I thought it would be fun to do."

I narrow my eyes at him. "Real childish, Jamie."

He holds up my phone. "Hey, at least I saved your phone."

He then snaps a picture of me in the pool. He also had his own phone out and snaps a picture with his.

"Don't you dare post that to social media," I snarl at him.

"What if I do?"

"I will bury you six feet under this snow."

Jamie laughs. "I would like to see you try, O'Connor. Although you and I both know you will never do that."

He is right. I wouldn't end up doing it. I will have to find another way to get back at him.

"Well, goodnight, O'Connor." He turns around and places my phone on the lawn chair. He turns back to me. "I will leave this right here for you. I will see you tomorrow."

He walks away, leaving me alone in the pool. I get out and grab my phone, letting out a frustrating scream.

"I hate you, Jamie Jackson," I call out to him as he was leaving the pool area.

He turns back to me. "I hate you too, Candice O'Connor."

And without another word, he leaves the pool. Instead of walking back to the entertainment area, I text my mom that I was heading back to the room. There was no way I was going back in there. Plus, this cold was stabbing me like a thousand knives, and I need to get out of these clothes before I freeze to death.

I will get Jamie back for this. He will pay for ever messing with me from the moment he snatched that pencil out of my hand in kindergarten.

# Chapter Nine

Jamie Jackson has got to be the biggest jerk on this planet. I mean, honestly, out of all the kids in our class back in kindergarten, why did he choose to pick me as his enemy? Was I different to the other kids? The only thing different about me was I was the *only* kid with red hair. But why pick on me because of that? From the very first day of school, I had always been friendly to my classmates, and that's included Jamie. Yet, he had chosen not to be friends with me.

I keep thinking about all of this as I shiver my way back to the lodge and head up to my room. I light up the fire and warm myself against it. I head to my room to find my pyjamas before heading to the bathroom to strip off my wet clothes and take a shower to wash off the chlorine. It was a good thing he had thought about my phone. I would have killed him if he had pushed me into the pool with it.

Ugh, why is this guy like this around me? I can't wait until the end of summer where he can buzz off to whatever college he is going to. Even though there's less than six months until we graduate, I will most likely still see him around town during the summer.

I was freshly cleaned and out of my wet clothes, which I had hung up near the fire, in hope they will dry in time by the time my family comes back up to the room. The last thing I wanted was to explain to them was why my clothes were soaking wet and what I was doing near the pool. Gabriella is the one I wanted to avoid these questions the most from, because I know she will start asking what was going on between Jamie and me. I mean, she can clearly see that *nothing* is going on between us. We could never be lovers. We hate each other so much that sometimes it's exhausting to come up with sarcastic comments or pranks to get back at each other. And what made him want to push me into the pool, I don't know. Jerk.

I made myself a hot chocolate, disappointed that I wasn't able to drink mine earlier. Hannah most likely would have drunk it. I sit down beside the fire, sipping the hot drink while on the phone with Allegra.

"I really can't believe the jerk did that to me," I tell her. "I mean, who would lead someone outside to apologize for something they did earlier, and then lead you to the pool and push you in?" I shake my head. "Jamie Jackson is unbelievable."

"Maybe you should seek revenge," Allegra suggests.

"Like what?" I take a sip of my drink.

"I don't know. Something to make you leave you alone for the rest of this trip."

As soon as she says it, the idea hits me.

"Yes! Of course!" I cry. "Allegra, thank you. Jamie is going to pay for this."

"What are you going to do?"

"I'm going to make him disappear."

As soon as I get off the phone with Allegra, I start planning. I drink my hot chocolate as I stare at the fire, thinking of all the ways to make him disappear. It wasn't like I could get a magic wand and wave it at him, say some kind of spell and zap him with the wand to make him vanish. No, I had to do something that would definitely get him away from me long enough for me to enjoy the rest of this trip with my family.

A smile curls across my lips when I figure out exactly what I was going to do. I have no idea how I am going to do it, but I will find a way.

When I finish my drink, I check my clothes. They were slightly damp, and that should be good enough. Maybe I will hang them up on the back of the chairs in the dining room tonight, and by tomorrow morning they should be dry. Mom had texted me to let me know they were on the way up. I remove the damp clothes and hang them on the back of the chairs just as my family walked through the front door. We talk a bit before calling it a night, Hannah telling me everything that happened after I had left with Jamie. Gabriella kept watching me without saying a word, like she was trying to figure out what Jamie and I had gotten up to while we were alone. If only she knew, would she still be saying I had a crush on him?

As I lay my head to rest on my pillow for the night, I smile, not being able to wait tomorrow on what I plan to do to Jamie Jackson. He was going to be sorry.

* * *

The next morning once I was all ready to go head down to

breakfast with my family, I couldn't wait to confront Jamie. His family is already in the dining room when we enter. Grabbing a plate, I stroll over to him where he was filling his plate with slices of bacon, his plate already had two slices of toast, two sausages, and scrambled eggs. He looks my way.

He puts the tongs he was using down. "Good morning, O'Connor. How was your swim last night?" He smirks.

He reaches for another pair of tongs and picks up a hash brown and places it on his plate.

Instead of answering him, I say, "What are you up to today?"

He picks up another hash brown but doesn't put it on his plate. Instead, he puts it on my empty plate. It wasn't something I was planning to have this morning, but I take it without arguing.

"I'm going to hit the slopes early before this snowstorm is predicted to hit around noon," Jamie says. He puts the tongs down, turning back to me. "Why do you ask? Are you trying to make sure you stay away from me? It's not going to work, O'Connor. I'm telling you. I can guarantee that I will be somewhere on the slope near you, no matter how hard you try to avoid me. So you need to get used to it that we are hanging out together for the holidays."

Getting smart with me first thing in the morning. Nice.

But he won't be smart for long once I get him back for what he did last night.

And I'm going to have to plan it quickly before we are hit with the snowstorm predicted to hit us around noon. Dad had gotten an email this morning from the resort manager that the ski resort will remain open, but the staff will be monitoring the wind speeds in case the storm gets worse and they have to close the slopes for the day. So hopefully this storm holds up long enough to let me do what I need to do, and then it was free to come.

"Look, I haven't forgotten that idiotic stunt you pulled on me last night," I say.

Jamie raises an eyebrow. "Idiotic, huh? I wasn't aware that pushing you into the pool was idiotic."

I roll my eyes. "Whatever. But let's put it aside. I was thinking we could go snowboarding together today."

Jamie looks at me, surprised. "You want us to go snowboarding together?"

As soon as it says this, I realize it sounded like a ridiculous idea. Jamie and I snowboarding together. Yesterday was bad enough, and today can't be any better. Yet, if I wanted to go with my plan, I had no choice but to go up onto the slopes with him. And if he doesn't want to go with me, then I will have to come up with Plan B.

But knowing Jamie, he will agree to do this. Anything to annoy me later.

I nod. "Yes, I do."

"Are you sick, O'Connor?"

I roll my eyes. It can't be that bad for asking him to do something with me, right? Okay, who am I kidding? It's bad. We are enemies. Enemies don't hang out with each other.

"Answer the question, Jamie. Do you want to go snowboarding with me or not?"

"What's the catch if I do?"

"On the plane you said we needed to make a truce, right? Especially if we are going to be at this resort together for a week."

He nods. "Yes, I remember."

"So, let's make a truce. Let's spend the day with each other, and we must try not to irritate each other."

This is the dumbest thing I have ever had to ask Jamie, and I don't know how I was going to do this. Who am I kidding that this will even work? I should abandon the plan.

Jamie nods. "Okay. I will meet up with you later."

Without another word, he wanders over to his family.

I watch him for a moment, not believing that I've just asked Jamie Jackson to hang out with me. Even when we get back to school and Miss Fields was to ask us if we could work together on the winter dance, I would not want to be anywhere near the guy.

But if everything goes according to plan, once on top of one of the slopes, I will be able to make sure he does leave me alone for the rest of the vacation.

\* \* \*

"This morning you girls can do your own activities, and then about eleven o'clock we will meet for lunch," Dad tells us as we walk out of the locker room where we store our rental ski equipment. "Then after lunch, what do you say we do something together as a family?"

"Can we play in the snow, making snow angels?" Hannah asks.

Dad smiles. "Of course, Hannah."

"Honey, don't forget about the snowstorm that is predicted today," Mom pointed out.

Dad nods. "Right. Thanks for reminding me about that. I don't know how bad this snowstorm will be, but if it gets too bad, we will head back to the lodge. The resort will let us know if the storm gets worse."

Dad allows Gabriella and I to go off to do our own activity. I walk with Gabriella, who was heading over to the learning how to ski area.

"How is it going with learning to ski?" I ask.

Gabriella nods with a smile. "Good. I thought it was going to be hard, but my instructor said I'm picking it up quickly."

"That's good."

"You should come with me."

I shake my head. "I would, but I'm more of a snowboarder."

"Okay."

"Maybe before the trip ends we can go snowboarding together?"

Gabriella smiles. "I would love that."

Gabriella and I go our separate ways. I head over to the chair lift Jamie had suggested we meet at. He is there, looking around. When he spots me, he smirks.

"It's good to see you again, O'Connor," he says.

I roll my eyes when I see him. I can't believe I'm doing this. Any other day I would not request to do an activity with him, but today I am. This plan better work.

Jamie and I sit on the chair. As it moves up the mountain, I keep my head straight without looking at him. As it goes higher, I could see dark clouds in the distance. It must be the snowstorm. Hopefully I can work on my plan before the storm hits us at noon.

"How much time do you think we have to snowboard today before the snowstorm hits us?" Jamie asks. I shrug. "I don't know. A few hours maybe."

"I hope so. My brother said the ski resort will remain open, but some slopes may close and the chair lifts will be out of order. If the storm gets real bad, then they have to close it down for the rest of the day until the snow stops."

Can he stop talking and let me enjoy this ride up?

"So, Christmas is tomorrow," he goes on. "What plans do you have with your family?"

I shrug. "I don't know yet. My parents haven't discussed it with us. We aren't doing presents this year. So maybe we will spend the day as a family. There's a Christmas market that we have talked about going to. My dad said the dining room will be open for a special Christmas dinner."

"Yum."

"What about your family?" Not that I really care, but I knew the polite thing to do was ask.

"My mom put up a small tree in our room, beside the fireplace. In the morning we will open presents."

For the rest of the ride up we talk about Christmas, and then Jamie brought up the winter dance, asking me if I had come up with any ideas for decorations yet. Of course I haven't even thought about it since school let out for winter break. Even Gabriella hasn't discussed it with me. Maybe she will talk to me about it once we get back home.

As soon as we were at top of the mountain, I get off the chair. My natural instinct was to move as far away as I could from him, but then I remember my plan and move away from the chair lifts with him at my side.

*Just a little while longer with him and then you can ditch him*, I tell myself. *You can do this, Candice.*

"So, how are we going to do this?" Jamie asks me. "Do you want to race down?"

"Actually, I thought that maybe we should go for a walk."

Jamie looks at me strangely. "A walk? Where? I thought

you said you wanted to snowboard."

"I do. But first I want to take a walk."

Jamie stares at me for what seems like forever before shrugging. "Okay. If you say so."

"Good. Come on."

We unstrap our feet from the snowboards. I lead the way, walking away from the slope towards the trees.

"You know, if you wanted to go for a walk, we could have gone snowshoeing instead. Why don't we go and rent them?" Jamie suggests.

"Maybe because I don't want to go snowshoeing."

"But we might as well if we are going for a walk. It will be easier to walk in the snowshoes than it would be in these boots."

I sigh. He really doesn't know how to shut up.

"Just shut up and follow me," I tell him.

We get to the tree line and I look back at the slope with the other skiers, hoping no one has seen us here. I didn't want us to be seen or my plan will be ruined.

"Is there something you want to tell me, O'Connor?" Jamie asks me, stopping next to me and putting the snowboard to rest beside him.

I turn my attention to him. "Why do you think there is something I need to tell you?"

"Well, for one thing you are leading me here." He casually leans up against a tree trunk. "Tell me something, O'Connor. Are you wanting a little private time with me?" He wiggles his eyebrows at me.

I look at him, disgusted. "Ew, seriously?"

I roll my eyes and turn, heading towards the trees.

Jamie follows me. "I'm kidding, O'Connor!"

I turn back to him once we are away from everyone. "What makes you think I even want to be alone with you?"

Jamie gestures his arms around at his surroundings. "Well, no one is around. So that makes us alone."

I shake my head. "Keep dreaming, Jamie."

"Do you have a crush on me?"

I laugh. First Gabriella, and now Jamie is asking me this. "Yeah, right. What makes you think I have a crush on you?"

"Well, do you? Come on, O'Connor, you can admit it to me."

"No! I don't have a crush on you."

I turn away, walking ahead until I come to the ski resort boundary. A yellow sign attached to a black and yellow stripe pole read that past this area was not patrolled and we risk being in an area that was likely to have avalanches. Normally I would listen to the sign and head back, but today I didn't care. I was going beyond it, in hope that Jamie will follow me. We couldn't get in trouble being here if no one saw us, right?

I cross the boundary line.

"Ah, Candice, the resort is back that way," Jamie points out.

"I know, but I don't want to go back to the resort yet."

"Are you seriously leaving the resort area?"

I turn around to face him, where he stood at the sign, not daring to cross it. "Yes, I'm serious about leaving the area."

"We can't leave this area, Candice."

His voice is serious as he said it. Like he was afraid that if we leave this area, he will be in trouble. I have never known him to be worried about being in trouble. At school he was carefree and lived up to a reputation, didn't worry about being in trouble for anything. But like the sign said, there was no one patrolling this area.

"Of course we can," I say. "You aren't afraid about being in trouble, are you Jamie?"

"It's not that, Candice. Like the sign says, it's not patroled, and we risk being in an avalanche area. Also, there's a snowstorm coming, and we really shouldn't be too far from the resort."

This I knew was true, and I have thought about the snowstorm. I didn't want to be stuck out here when it comes. But there was still time to lure Jamie out here, and get back to the resort before the storm comes. He will be lost in the wilderness and I can enjoy the rest of the vacation without him around.

"We will be fine, Jamie," I tell him. "I'm going to go for a walk. I promise you I won't go too far and we will be back before the storm hits. Are you coming?"

He stares at me for a long time before looking over his shoulder. When it showed no one was coming for us, Jamie steps across the boundary.

"Just so you know, I'm only coming along to make sure you are safe," he tells me.

I smile. "Great."

# Chapter Ten

I didn't know how far I should go from the resort. I didn't want to go too far and get lost. But somehow, I needed to ditch Jamie and head back. The storm was getting closer, and if I don't head back now, I will be stuck out here.

"Besides going for a walk, are we going backcountry snowboarding?" Jamie asks me. "Is that what we are doing out here?"

Backcountry snowboarding was something I hadn't thought of doing when I lead Jamie off the resort. While no one could stop you from leaving the ski boundary so you could backcountry ski, it wasn't exactly recommended. Not without some adventure tour who did that kind of activity, or you had the right training for avalanche safety and special gear.

I stop walking, putting my snowboard down to rest. Why did I agree to do this? Maybe I should have considered snowshoeing like Jamie had suggested so I didn't have to carry the board with me.

"You are welcome to do so if you want to," I tell him.

Jamie stops walking and stands next to me, setting his board down too.

"If I want to? Candice, what are we really doing out here? I'd rather snowboard at the resort where it's safe."

"Well then, why did you follow me out here? No one asked you to."

"I followed you to make sure you are safe. Anything could happen to you out here if you are alone. What if something serious happens and you can't get back to the resort? No one is going to know you are out here, Candice."

It was strange to hear him call me by my first name and not by my surname. I have heard him say my first name a few times, but this time it just felt strange. Using my first name was to show me he was frustrated and worried about me that he couldn't be bothered to be using my surname.

"Well, no one asked you to come out here." I point to in what I think is the direction of the resort. "You are free to go back."

"And leave you out here alone?" He shakes his head. "Not a chance, Candice."

"I don't need you to baby-sit me."

Jamie laughs hysterically. "If you don't want to be baby-sat, then don't act like a child."

I frown at him, resting my hands on my hips. "Who are you to call me a child?"

"I'm sure anyone would call you a child with the way you are acting."

I shake my head. "You are such a jerk."

I grab my snowboard and began walking away. As I do, it starts to snow lightly.

"I'm a jerk? At least I'm not the stupid one who decided to leave the resort. Tell me the real reason why we are out here."

I groan. He really isn't going to leave me alone about this. There is no way I could tell him the real reason why I lead us both out here. Just so I didn't have to explain myself, I kept walking. How I was going to ditch Jamie out here, I wasn't sure. Somehow, I need to sneak away back to the resort without him, or this whole plan will be pointless.

I hear Jamie's footsteps in the snow behind me as he tries to catch up to me.

"Slow down, Candice, and let's talk."

"I don't want to talk to you," I call over my shoulder.

"You don't want to talk to me?" Jamie snickers. "Funny, Candice, because you are the one who spoke to me in the first place and wanted me to come snowboarding with you. Then you lead me out here to go for a walk, and decide you don't want to talk to me? Nice, Candice. Real nice. Are you still going to tell me what we are doing out here?"

*Can you just stop talking?* I want to say.

I look around me. There's a tree line to my right and open mountain ranges to my left. Maybe I should make a run for it in the trees, hide out there until I lose Jamie and then head back to the resort. I glance up at the grey clouds above me as the snow begins to get heavy. I should really ditch Jamie now and head back to the resort before the snowstorm gets worse. At least the snow will cover up my tracks so he can't follow me.

It's now or never.

Without looking behind me, I run towards the trees.

"Where are you going, Candice?" Jamie yells after me.

I don't dare to look back to see if he is following me. I run into the forest, but not too deeply that I couldn't find my way out again. When I was sure I had lost Jamie, I hid behind a tree trunk, and rest my back against it to wait.

"Candice?" he yells. "Candice, answer me! This isn't funny! Candice!"

I stay quiet for a moment. The only sound I could hear was Jamie's voice, calling for me. Amongst his voice was the wind, whistling through the trees. Now would be a good time to get out of here and make it back to the resort before the storm gets worse. The last thing I needed was for this storm to turn into a blizzard. I would be screwed then.

I glance around the trunk to see if I could see Jamie anywhere, but all I could see is an empty forest. He keeps calling out my name. He can call me as much as he wants, but I wasn't going to answer.

Goodbye Jamie Jackson. It was nice knowing you.

Not.

When I felt like the coast was clear and I was able to make my escape, I move away from the trunk and start making my way back in the direction I had come.

Only I didn't make it very far.

My foot hits the tree roots. I hit the snow, my snowboard flying out of my grip. As I go to sit up, I feel a sharp pain go through my right ankle.

No, no, no! This wasn't supposed to happen! If I sprain my ankle now, I was not going to make it back to the resort before the storm gets worse. And if Jamie finds me, this whole plan with leading him out here and getting lost was going to be a waste of time.

Jamie calls out to me again. Still not answering him back, I slowly get to my feet, only I couldn't put weight on my foot. Great. This is what I needed right now. Biting down on my lip,

I wince as I stumble over to the snowboard just a few yards from me. But I didn't get far and had to sit down.

"Candice?"

I close my eyes and sigh. Can he stop calling my name? I don't want him to find me. I want him to disappear and leave me alone forever.

I open my eyes again, resting a hand on my ankle. Why did I think it was wise to lure Jamie out here again?

"Candice?"

His voice is close this time and when I look up, I see him hurrying over to me.

"Candice, are you okay?" He puts his snowboard down and kneels in the snow next to me.

"I tripped. I think I sprained my ankle."

"Can you walk?"

I shake my head. "No. I can't put any weight on it."

"Okay, well we should get back to the resort and get first aid to look at your ankle. I don't think it's wise to look at it right here now. We need to get back fast before the storm worsens."

He picks up our snowboards, then helps me up, putting an arm around my waist to steady me. Half of me was tempted to tell him to remove his arm from around my waist, but I knew without him right now, I wouldn't be able to make it back to the resort with my sprained ankle. To hold more of my balance, I put my arm around his shoulders.

We didn't say anything to each other at first, wandering slowly through the forest. It didn't help that the snow had covered our tracks, stopping us from finding our way out. I know I hadn't gone too deeply into the forest. Or maybe I had without knowing. Why did I go too far in here, turning corners in hopes of losing Jamie?

"Which way are we supposed to go?" Jamie asks me.

"I don't know," I answer. I strain my brain to remember which way, but all I could think about is the pain shooting up my ankle.

"You don't know? Why did you lead us out here then if you don't know which way?"

"Oh, so you are blaming me for the reason why we are lost?"

"Like I said, you are the one who led us out here."

I push Jamie off me. "Well, no one asked you to follow me."

*But I wanted you to follow me*, I silently say to myself.

"Yeah, well imagine what would have happened if I didn't follow you. How would you have gotten back with your sprained ankle?"

I laugh at this because there would have been no way I would have sprained my ankle if I *didn't* lead him out here. If he hadn't come onto this same trip as me, I wouldn't have to come up with an idea to get rid of him so he leaves me alone.

"Why are you laughing at this, Candice?" he asks. "If we can't find our way back, we are going to freeze to death out here during the snowstorm. We have to hope it doesn't get worse and turn into a blizzard. And there's no cell service out here for us to call for help to come rescue us."

"Oh trust me. I wouldn't be out here either if I didn't have to figure out how to make you disappear for the rest of this vacation."

Jamie stares at me. I lean on a tree trunk for support as I stand on my good foot so I didn't put any pressure on my ankle.

"Wait. Did you just trick me into following you out here so you can lose me, then I get lost on trying to find my way back to the resort? Meanwhile, you are back at the resort, having the time of your life while I am out here, probably freezing to death and worrying where you are, thinking that you could be lost out here too?"

I don't answer.

Jamie is taken back by my silence. "Wow. I knew we were enemies, but I didn't think you would go out of your way to do something so selfish. How would you have felt if I had decided to lure you out here, ditch you, and go back to the resort to enjoy the rest of winter break without you around?"

When he says this back to me, it suddenly hits me that he is right. What was I thinking in wanting to lead Jamie out here and then ditch him, all because I wanted to enjoy the rest of my vacation without him? Even just going beyond the ski area boundary was dangerous. Anything could have happened to either of us like Jamie had told me when he advised me not to cross it. Now I have twisted my ankle, and we weren't going to be able to get back to the resort in this weather.

For a long time, Jamie and I stare at each other in silence, just the cold wind blowing through the trees. I shiver. We needed to get out of this weather.

Jamie shakes his head at me. "I can't believe you, Candice."

Standing here became awkward and uncomfortable. And I wish my hatred for Jamie Jackson didn't come to this.

"I'm sorry, Jamie," I say, forcing myself to look in his eyes to show him that I meant it.

He stares at me, watching me carefully like he was trying to figure me out, or if my apology was real. He shivers briefly, and then glances up in the sky.

He turns back to me. "We can stand here all day arguing about what you did, but right now we need to find shelter. If we stay here and argue, we will freeze. So let's try our best to get back to the resort, okay?"

I nod. "Okay."

Tucking the boards under our arms, we put our free arms around each other. Slowly we started moving in the direction we think is the right way.

"I'm really sorry for getting you into this mess, Jamie," I apologize again. "I was stupid to think this was such a great idea."

"It's okay. I guess it was payback for what I did last night to you when I pushed you in the pool."

"Why did you do it?"

"I don't know. It was something I thought would be fun to do."

I roll my eyes. "Yeah, trying not to freeze all the way back to your room is fun."

"How is your ankle?" Jamie asks instead of responding to my remark.

"Sore."

"When we get back to the resort, I will get you to first aid and they will take a look at your ankle."

"Thank you, Jamie... for helping me."

Ugh. I can't believe I'm actually thanking him for something. All my life I have never thanked him for anything.

"It's no problem, O'Connor. Just be glad I was out here with you."

# Chapter Eleven

We move slowly through the snow, shivering so much that our teeth chatter. We still haven't even made it out of the forest. I don't even remember running this far in when I ran from Jamie. I was only meant to run a short distance, hide from him, and then go back the way I came. But then I had to go and twist my ankle. I could have gotten out before the snow had fallen more, or before he had found me.

It didn't help that our foot prints in the snow was now covered up by the falling snow, completely wiping away our path that was our only way of getting back to the resort. My mind was spinning with thoughts, like what my parents were going to say when they discover I'm not at the resort. I can definitely imagine how much trouble I will be in. I will mostly likely be grounded for wandering off like I did, all because I just wanted a guy I hated so much to disappear for the rest of the vacation. Yay, what a great end to the year knowing I will be grounded into the New Year.

Damn it. Why did I get myself into this mess?

On top of that, why did this forest feel so much like a maze that you couldn't find the way out?

"How did we go so far into the forest and then not find our way out of this?" I ask.

"Don't ask me this question," Jamie hisses. "I'm not the one who had ran into it, hoping I could somehow ditch someone out here."

"Look, I'm sorry, okay?"

"Whatever, Candice. Just don't bother to do any more of your apologies until we get back to the resort."

The wind feels like it is getting stronger and more snow is falling. It's then I spot something in the distance. I squint my eyes to what looked like a building. It couldn't be the resort, but perhaps it was someone's house near the resort.

I nod towards the building. "Jamie, up ahead. I think it is a building."

"I see it. Come on. Let's head towards there and get out of this storm. Maybe we can get help."

We make our way towards it, glad that something was nearby for us to seek shelter in. I'm pretty sure I hadn't led us too far from the resort, so maybe this building was not far from it. Once the storm is over, we will be able to head back to the resort.

When we are closer, we see it's a log cabin. No lights were on.

"Do you think anyone is home?" I ask Jamie as we walk up the front steps.

"Hopefully."

Jamie walks me over to the porch swing and sits me down. He walks over to the front door. There's a wreath hung on the door. He knocks on it a couple of times, but no one answers. He then peeks through the window.

"It doesn't look like anyone is home," Jamie tells me.

My heart sinks with disappointment. If no one is home, what are we going to do? We can't stay out in this storm. We will freeze to death if we don't find shelter or someplace warm, especially if the storm worsens.

I do not want to die out here with my worst enemy.

"What are we going to do?" I ask him.

He shrugs. "Well, we most definitely can't stay out here."

Jamie tries the door. I expected the handle to jiggle, but it opens in one swift moment. He turns to me. "Well, that was easy."

My eyes widen at the thought that whoever lived here left their front door open for anyone to walk in. "Who would leave their doors unlocked like that?"

"Well, I guess if you live in a cabin in the middle of the woods, you can leave the doors unlocked. The only thing that will be breaking in are animals." He walks over to me, grabbing his snowboard and then helping me off the porch swing. "Come on, let's get you inside."

We move across the porch slowly, and head inside. Jamie rests his snowboard against the wall near the door, while still holding onto me, and closes the door. He switches on the light switch, and the room lights up.

"Great," Jamie says. "We still have power."

He takes my snowboard and rests it against the wall next to his. We then take off our jackets and place them on the coat hooks on wall next to the door.

I glance around the cabin. We were standing in the living room. To our left is a fireplace, a brown couch with a blanket folded neatly on top. A coffee table was in front of the couch. A bookshelf was against one wall. And there was a Christmas tree in one corner. No television though.

To our right was an open door that led to the bedroom, a bathroom next to it, and the kitchen at the other end. Whoever lived here, lived a simple life.

*How long we will be here for?* I wonder. I hope it won't be for too long. I don't want to stay here alone with Jamie. No doubt we will end up killing each other before this storm is over.

Jamie leads me over to the couch and makes me sit down. He grabs the blanket and wraps it around me. He walks over to the fireplace, adding some logs that's in a pile beside it. At least we didn't have to go outside in this weather to grab firewood. He grabs the gas lighter that's sitting on top of the fireplace, and lights it. As soon as it's lit, I can feel the heat from the fire. With the fire burning, it made the cabin feel nice and cosy.

"Do you think whoever lives here minds that we are here?" I ask, wrapping the blanket tightly around me.

Jamie stands up, placing the gas lighter back on top of the fireplace. He turns around to face me, shrugging. "Maybe. I'm sure if they come back home they won't mind if we tell them what we are doing here. I'm sure they will understand." He nods towards me. "How is your ankle?"

I put my leg up onto the couch, and as I did, a sharp pain goes through my ankle. I wince, resting my hand on it like it would somehow stop the pain. But it doesn't, throbbing.

Jamie hurries over to me. "Let me see your ankle."

He sits on the other end of the couch and rests my foot in his lap. He takes off my boot and sock. I shiver as his fingers touch my skin. The thought of him touching me made me want to pull away, and then wash my skin with soap to make all traces of him go away. He examines my foot carefully.

"Your ankle is swollen and a bruise is forming." He looks up at me. "Stay here and I will get you some ice. It's a sprain. Just keep your foot up and you should be okay."

He gets up, carefully placing my foot back on the couch. He strolls towards the kitchen, opening the freezer door. He returns with a bag of frozen vegetables wrapped with a paper towel. Jamie sits back down on the couch, resting my foot on his lap again. I'm not even prepared when he puts the towel against my ankle. The cold makes me shiver.

Jamie looks up at me as he holds the bag into place. His brown eyes are full of concern, and it was something I never expected to see in him. "How does that feel?"

I nod. "It feels good. Thank you, Jamie."

"You're welcome. Just sit here with it for twenty minutes. I'm going to search the house to see if I can find a first aid kit. I might also find some candles in case we lose power from the storm."

He carefully gets off from the couch again, and leaves the room. I hear him banging cupboard drawers in the bathroom, until he finally emerges with a bandage in his hand.

"There's no first aid kit, but I found a bandage. I will wrap it on your ankle later once you are finished with the ice." He sets it down on the coffee table.

"Okay," I answer.

"Is there anything else you need before I go searching for candles?"

"Can I have a glass of water, please?"

Jamie walks back to the kitchen, banging cupboards and then I hear the kitchen sink. He walks back over to me with the glass of water in hand. I thank him and take a sip. Before he leaves, he tells me to call out to him if I needed him. He leaves me alone with the nice warm fire. Outside, the wind howls.

While he goes off looking around the house, I decided to check my phone. I can't imagine how crazy my parents are going in wondering where I am. Just the thought if it is making me feel stupid for coming up with this childish prank only to get rid of the boy I hate so much. I might as well call them and let them know I'm okay, and that I'm somewhere in the mountains in some cabin in the middle of nowhere.

Only when I went to call, there was no signal on my cell.

"Jamie!"

Jamie hurries back in the living room, holding a box of candles and a flashlight. "What is it, O'Connor?"

I wave my cell phone at him. "We have no cell service."

Jamie looks at me like it's no big deal. "I know. We are out of cell phone range."

I put my phone down on my lap. "Seriously? How are we going to contact anyone to let them know where we are?"

Jamie shrugs. "I don't know. I'm sure whoever lives here will help us out. They probably have something they can contact the outside world with."

"This is crazy! We are in the twenty first century! It's 2021, almost 2022. How can there not be a signal in the mountains by now?"

"You see why I told you it wasn't a very good idea to leave the ski resort boundary?"

I frown. I put my glass of water down on the floor beside the couch. I then look back at him. "Oh, I get it. It's my fault that there is no signal."

"That's not what I said, Candice." He comes around and put the candles and flashlight on the table. He turns back to me. "I told you it wouldn't be a good idea to leave the boundary, but you didn't listen to me. What for? So you can lead me out into the middle of nowhere, abandon me, and head back to the resort where you can enjoy the rest of the holidays without me around?" He scoffs, gesturing around the cabin. "Look at where we are, Candice, all because of your stupid decision." He puts his arms down. "You are lucky it was just a snowstorm out there, and not a blizzard. We would have died out there if we hadn't stumbled upon this cabin. Did you ever think about what would have happened if we got stuck out here and couldn't get back to the resort? Maybe we wouldn't be stuck in a snowstorm. Maybe something else could have happened."

He was right. It was stupid of me to even come up with this plan to get rid of him. It didn't turn out the way I had planned. Instead of getting away from him, I was now trapped in this cabin with him until the storm subsides.

You know what? Who cares if there is a snowstorm out there? I'm going to brave the storm and get out of here. I was not going to stay here any longer. Not with *him*.

I grab my sock and boot from the floor where Jamie had put it, and remove the bag of frozen peas from my ankle, slipping on my sock.

Jamie stands there, watching me. "What are you doing?"

I put my boot on next. "What does it look like I'm doing? I'm leaving."

Jamie shakes his head at me. "You can't leave, Candice."

I do my laces, asking, "Why not?"

"You know very well why, Candice. There's a snowstorm out there."

I look up at him, frowning. "So what? At least I don't have to be stuck in here with you."

I expected Jamie to say something smart back, but instead he just stands there with his hands in his pockets, watching me carefully. We keep eye contact for a few short moments before I make the first move. I stood up, wincing as I put weight on my foot. Jamie is about to come over to me, but I held up my hands.

"No. Don't come near me. I don't need your help."

He stands still, keeping his eyes on me.

I turn and head towards the door, limping my way there. I could hardly put the weight on my foot, but I force myself to. My ankle is throbbing by the time I reach the door. I grab my jacket and put it on.

But before I could get out the door, Jamie grabs me, spinning me around and then pushes me up against the door. The fast movement causes a sharp pain to shoot up my leg. I let out a cry.

"I can't let you go out there, Candice," he tells me, his hands firmly on my shoulders as he holds me against the door and against my own will.

I push against his chest, but he doesn't move. "Get off me, you jerk!"

"Not until you promise me that you aren't going out there. If you leave to go out in that storm, you will get hypothermia. You aren't going to last long out there."

"Why do you care if I get hypothermia or not?"

"Look, I may be some jerk. But I'm not heartless. I'm not going to let you go out there and freeze to death trying to make your way back to the resort with a sprained ankle."

"Well, at least it's better than being stuck in here with you."

Jamie snickers. "Yeah, well I don't exactly want to be stuck in here with you either. It's Christmas Eve, and I rather spend it with my family instead of you."

"Same goes for me."

"Well, then you should have thought twice about leaving the resort boundary. You would be back in your room with your family, spending this terrible Christmas Eve with them."

Jamie is right. We would be back at the ski lodge, riding out the storm in our rooms. My family and I would be in the room next to the fireplace. We would play games to keep our minds off the storm. Every Christmas Eve, my Mom makes hot chocolate with whipped cream, marshmallows, and chocolate shavings on top. She always made it as a special Christmas treat before we headed off to bed. She also made it as a special treat before dinner with Christmas cookies.

Thinking about it made me miss my family, wondering if I will ever get out of here and I will be able to see them again. Crying in front of Jamie was not what I wanted, but I couldn't help it as the tears fell, making me hate myself for doing something so stupid all because of my hatred towards Jamie.

Jamie pulls me into a hug, rubbing a hand along my back to soothe me. I cry into his shoulder.

"It's okay, Candice," he says. "It's okay."

"I'm sorry, Jamie," I say, "I'm sorry for acting selfish and trying to vanish you. I'm sorry for getting us into this mess."

Jamie pushes me gently off him, and takes my wrist. He leads me slowly back over to the couch, careful not to hurt my ankle. He sits me down before sitting beside me. He wipes my tears away.

"It's going to be alright, Candice," he tells me. "Once the snow stops, we will figure out how to get back to the resort."

I nod, sniffing as I wipe my nose. I can't believe I'm crying in front of the boy I hate. "It's Christmas Eve. My Mom makes this special hot chocolate for us. She is probably making them right now back at the lodge, and I'm not there to have one."

Jamie rests a hand on my knee. "Well, tell me how to make it, and I will see if there's any ingredients in the kitchen that I could use to make this hot chocolate."

I was surprise to hear Jamie say this. I expected him to laugh and tell me it serves me right for missing out on it. "You will make it?"

Jamie smiles at me. It wasn't a smirk, it was an actual smile. "I will go and make one for the both of us. Hot chocolate sounds good right now."

He gets off the couch, telling me to put the frozen peas back on my ankle, and disappears to the kitchen.

# Chapter Twelve

The hot chocolate Jamie had made was delicious, even if it wasn't the same way my mom would make it. There was no cream or chocolate shavings to put on top. But Jamie did manage to find a bag of marshmallows in the pantry, placing three of them in the mug. The sweet and creamy beverage helped me to feel a little better about being away from my family and being trapped inside a cabin with someone I hated.

Jamie and I sit on the couch for a long time in silence as we sip our drinks, listening to the cracking sound of the fire and the howling wind outside. I wasn't even sure how long we have been here for.

"How long do you think this storm will last for?" I break the silence.

Jamie keeps his eyes ahead on the fire. "I don't know. A couple of hours maybe."

"I feel bad being in someone's home, eating their food and using their firewood that they worked hard on chopping."

"Same here. But I'm sure they will be okay with us being here to seek shelter. They wouldn't want us to freeze to death out there."

"Where do you think the owner is?"

Jamie shrugs. "Maybe they went into town and got caught up in the storm, and couldn't get back up here."

That was a possibility, and I hope we will be gone by then. I make a note to myself to leave a message behind for the owner to let them know that we had seek shelter here during the storm. That way when they do come home, they wouldn't think someone invaded their home. I hope this storm ends soon because I really don't want to be stuck here longer than I have to with Jamie. I'm sure he doesn't want to be stuck with me either.

I keep sipping my drink, wanting to avoid Jamie as much as I could. Instead, I think about my parents. I can imagine how insane they must be going through with worry, wondering where I am. I'm sure once my phone gains a signal, I will be able to see exactly how many missed calls I would have from Dad. I knew that once Jamie and I get out of here, I will most likely be grounded for the rest of the winter break, maybe even longer. I hope I won't be grounded all the way up to the winter dance. I wanted to be a part of it as it's my last year of high school, and attending this dance was important for my senior year.

I wonder if there's a search party looking for us right now, or would they wait until the storm is over.

I sip the last of my hot chocolate, a brief sadness washing over me as now I couldn't avoid Jamie. I would have to make conversation eventually.

"Hey, are you hungry?" Jamie asks me as he place his mug

onto the coffee table.

My stomach grumbles as he mentions this. With everything that has happened, lunch hadn't been on our minds. It was just an hour after midday.

I force myself to look at him and nod. "Yes, I'm hungry."

"I'm going to make us something. But before I do, I will wrap up your ankle."

He removes the frozen peas from my ankle. He places the bag on the table and takes the bandage he had placed on the table earlier. Holding onto my mug with both hands, I watch as Jamie carefully puts my foot on his lap. His warm hands brush my skin that was cold from the ice.

"The swelling has gone down a bit," he says. "I will bandage it up and then I will make us something to eat."

"Thank you, Jamie."

He gives me a small smile and then wraps up my ankle. When he finishes wrapping, he looks up at me. "That's not too tight?"

I shake my head. "No. It's fine."

Jamie slowly gets up and gently puts my foot down on the couch. He heads off to the kitchen to prepare lunch.

I sit there watching the fire as I cuddle up with the blanket. I keep my eyes on it and trying not to concentrate on the howling wind outside, reminding me of how stupid I am. I have never showed much hatred to anyone than what I showed towards Jamie Jackson. And now that hatred towards him lead me to doing something stupid, and I risked getting us both killed because of that decision.

In the kitchen I hear Jamie banging cupboard doors. The smell of toast fills the cabin. Jamie returns a few minutes later with two plates in his hand. He hands me a plate with two slices of grilled cheese. He sits down next to me with the same thing.

"Is grilled cheese okay?" he asks me.

I nod, biting into the sandwich. "It's fine. Thank you."

"Listen, I don't know how long we are going to be here for, but there isn't much food in the kitchen. It may not last long."

I wasn't sure what was worse. Being stuck here with Jamie, or potentially starving to death if we don't get out of here in time. But I'm overexaggerating because there is no way this storm will keep us trap in here forever. Right?

"I'm sure we aren't going to stay here for long," I say, even though I was secretly fearing we will be stuck in here forever.

"That all depends on how much snow is going to fall," Jamie tells me.

I don't even want to know how much snow is going to fall. It better not be a lot because I need to get out of this cabin and far away as possible from Jamie.

"We will be getting out of here by morning." I bite into my sandwich.

"I don't know. The weather looks awful out there. This storm is dumping a lot of snow."

I closed my eyes for a brief second. *Please don't say that.*

The thought of how much snow coming was terrifying. The last thing I wanted was to be stuck in this cabin for a couple of days with Jamie because we were snowed in. But I'm sure that's not going to happen. Tomorrow's Christmas. We will be out of here and we will be able to get back to the resort to spend this special day with our families. Jamie and I will forget any of this ever happened.

We ate our food in silence. When we are finish, Jamie took our plates and went to wash it.

"So, since we are stuck here for a while," Jamie says when he returns, "what should we do?"

I shrug. There wasn't anything I really wanted to do. Not with Jamie anyway.

"Come on, O'Connor. There must be something you would like to do. We are going to be in here for a long time."

I turn to him. "And what do you suggest we do?"

"We can play a game."

"I don't feel like playing a game. I just want to sit here and wait for the storm to be over."

"Like I had said, we could be waiting for a while for the storm to end. So we might as well pass the time."

"I'm fine."

Jamie stares at me for what seems like a long time. "You know, O'Connor, I know you hate me and you don't want to be stuck here with me. I'm not a fan of you either, but what choice do we have being here together until someone finds us, or until this storm stops. Can we put our differences aside for now?"

I look away from him, unsure how I was going to respond to his question. Our differences started the moment he snatched that pencil right out of my hand. Yeah, this all has gone through twelve years, and he was someone I will always hate. We were enemies for life. I can't even imagine putting our differences aside, not even for a second, let alone for the next few hours during this snowstorm, or even if we are stuck inside this cabin for a few days. I don't know how I'm going to get through this without committing a homicide.

And okay, twelve years is a very long time to hold a grudge on someone. Maybe we were six and he had done a childish thing that I shouldn't hate him for, but it's everything else he had done after that just to annoy me. It's like that day in kindergarten, out of everyone in our class who he could have taken that blue pencil from, he chose me. He knew he had struck a nerve in me, and had chosen from that day on to annoy me. Not just annoying me, but teasing me, especially about my hair. Now he wanted me to forget everything he had done, and put our differences aside so we can get through this together?

I swing my legs off the couch, wincing at the pain.

"Where are you going?" Jamie asks me.

"I'm going to the toilet," I answer.

I get up, and the moment I put weight on my ankle, I feel the pinch of the sharp pain.

Jamie gets up, ready to help me. "Here, let me help you."

I held up my hand. "No, I'm fine."

"Candice, let –"

"I'm fine, Jamie." The tone of my frustration causes him to back up.

We stare at each other. Without even having to say that I wanted him to stay away from him, he knows from the tone of my voice that I didn't want to sort out the differences between us. Not for him, and not for us.

I break away first, and limp towards the bathroom. Once I had locked the door, I let the tears roll down my cheeks. I didn't want to be alone here with Jamie. I wanted to be back at the resort with my parents and sisters. But who knows how long it was until we could get out of this cabin? And once we did get out, which way do we go to get to the resort? North? South? I'm not even sure what location we were at, or which way was north or south.

There's a knock on the door.

"Candice?"

I wipe my eyes, but don't answer him. I glance out the window, watching the snow fall outside. It showed no sign of stopping any time soon.

"Candice, please open up. Can you come out and we can talk?"

I wanted to laugh at this. Talk. Is that what he wanted? I'm sure it will lead us to fighting, and I didn't want to fight right now. I just wanted to go home.

When he realizes I wasn't going to open the door for him, he steps away from the door.

Now I just need the storm to stop so I could get out of here.

# Chapter Thirteen

If I could stay in the bathroom forever to avoid Jamie, I would. But I couldn't. The bathroom wasn't warm, and I wasn't going to freeze to death while I was in here. I had to face him eventually whether I liked it or not.

Quietly, I turn the knob. I peek out to see Jamie adding more wood to the fireplace. I sigh softly. What choice did I have to be out here with him when there were only four rooms in this house? I could also lock myself in the bedroom, but I will probably die of boredom. At least out here I get to talk to Jamie, even if I didn't want to. There wasn't much to do in here, so talking was the only option. I couldn't stay in the kitchen all day either. The living room was the only place I could be.

Jamie doesn't notice me as I limp out of the bathroom. But as I cross the room over to the Christmas tree, that's when he notices me. He doesn't say anything, and I don't make eye contact with him, but I could feel his eyes watching me carefully. I sit down beside the lit up Christmas tree. There were no presents around it, and I wonder if the people living here are spending Christmas somewhere else.

I sit down beside the tree, stretching out my sore ankle. I watch the colorful lights blink on and off. I wonder if the owners of the cabin knew they had left the Christmas tree lights on. Not that it mattered, because I like the lights. When I was little, the lights were the most fascinating thing I have ever seen. I found them relaxing to watch. Before Hannah was born, Gabriella and I had our own rooms, I used to have fairy lights hanging above my bed. Now that Gabriella and I share a room, I couldn't have lights above my bed. Instead, I hang them around the mirror on our vanity table.

I keep my eyes on the lights that I don't notice Jamie walking over to me until he wraps a blanket around me.

I glance up at him. He's tilting his head and making strong eye contact, waiting for me to say something. I give him a small smile. "Thanks."

He returns the smile and then sits down next to me beside the tree.

"When I was younger, I always found the tree comforting to sit next to whenever I was sad or wanted to relax," I say, looking at the tree instead of him. "I especially loved the fairy lights."

"When I was four, I didn't want to wait for Christmas," Jamie says, his eyes on the tree. "So a few days before Christmas, I got up before anyone and opened all of the presents, thinking they were all for me. I mean, I couldn't read so yeah I wasn't able to know which present had my name on it."

I turn to face him, my mouth slightly opened. "No. You didn't."

Jamie turns to me, chuckling. "I did. My parents were mad,

and my siblings hated me. I was four. I didn't understand why we had to wait until Christmas Day to open it. So for a few years after that, my parents decided not to put the presents under the tree until Christmas Eve after we had all gone to bed, just in case I tried to open them. They stopped punishing me for it when I was nine."

I laugh. "I can't believe you did that! I mean, I understand the impatience, but what kid does that?"

"Me, apparently. I kind of feel bad about it whenever I look back at it. But don't worry. It was a one-off thing. I never did it again. If I did, I probably wouldn't be invited for Christmas."

"Well, it looks like I'm ruining Christmas this year for both of our families. My parents will probably ground me until I'm fifty."

Jamie chuckles. "I'm pretty sure they won't ground you for that long."

True, I wouldn't be. I hardly got into trouble for anything, but I'm sure my parents would ground me for the rest of winter break.

"If you weren't stuck here with me, what would you be doing for Christmas Eve tonight?" I ask.

"Well, my brother has the night off tonight, so we were planning to go out to dinner."

"Sounds nice. How is everything with your family? You mentioned last night that your sister just found out she was pregnant."

He nods, turning to the tree. "Yeah. Estelle is pregnant. Six weeks."

I remember how last night he seemed upset about the whole pregnancy, or whatever was going on between him and his family.

"Are you excited about becoming an uncle?" I ask him.

He nods, turning back to me. "I am. But I feel my parents will just pay attention to the baby more than me. My parents always seem to put my brother and sister first. Sometimes I feel like they forget they have a third child. They don't really come to my hockey games, like they did when Estelle used to be a cheerleader or when my brother used to play sports."

I couldn't imagine my parents only paying attention to Gabriella and me, and then ignoring Hannah like she didn't exist. But my parents treated all of my sisters and me as equals, doing their very best to make sure they were there for activities we had. They were supportive in everything we did.

"I'm sorry you have to go through that," I say.

He shrugs, looking back at the tree. It was clear he didn't want to talk about this at all, so I didn't try to press any more questions. Besides, it's not like I even cared about what was going on within his life, but still, I feel for him for having his parents treat him like that. All this time I thought Jamie was a person who was so full of himself. But deep down he was someone struggling to have his parents take notice of him.

"If we weren't spending our Christmas vacation here at the resort, what would you be doing back at home?" I ask.

He turns back to me. "If we were spending Christmas at home instead of here, I would be helping my mom make gingerbread cookies. It was something she did with my siblings and I growing up. Also we baked a batch of choc-chip cookies, saving some to put out for Santa. What about you, Candice? What would you be doing?"

"If we were at home, we would be making gingerbread cookies too. And then later during the night before we headed off to bed, my mum will make her special hot chocolate."

Jamie smiles at me. "That sounds nice. I wish we had the chocolate shavings and whipped cream, then we could make it before we go to bed tonight. It sounds really nice. It's making me want some."

I laugh. "Well, maybe when we get out of here, I will definitely make you one."

I bite my tongue the moment I said it. What was I thinking to invite Jamie into my room back at the lodge to make Mom's special hot chocolate? Anyway, we may be acting nice to each other now, but I'm sure when we get out of here, we will go back to hating each other. It's what we do best.

I shiver briefly.

"Are you cold?" Jamie asks me.

"A little," I answer.

He stands up and then holds out his hand to me. "Come on, let's sit beside the fire."

I stare at his hand.

"I'm not going to bite you, O'Connor. Just take my hand."

I listen what he says and grab his hand. He then helps me up. I wince as I stand on my ankle. Slowly, we walk over to the fireplace, and sit down beside it, warming our hands up.

"This is nice and cosy," I say.

"It sure is. I couldn't think of a better way to spend Christmas than in a cosy cabin in the woods. How are you feeling now? Are you warm?"

I nod, pulling the blanket around me more. "I am."

"That's good."

"What about you? Aren't you going to wrap a blanket around you to keep warm?"

"Why, O'Connor, I didn't know you worried about me?"

I give him a serious look. "I'm serious, Jamie. As much as

I dislike you, we are stuck here together in the freezing cold."

"I'm fine. Don't worry about me."

We sit there for a moment in silence, staring at the fire.

"We are going to get out of here, O'Connor. Don't you worry."

\* \* \*

The snowstorm continues on a few hours later, and doesn't seem like it was going to stop any time soon. Each hour that went by, I worried more about what was happening at the lodge, what my parents must be going through wondering where I was. I couldn't imagine what Jamie's parents must be going through either.

So much for wishing Jamie would disappear for the rest of this vacation.

Even though I much rather be stuck with someone I liked, at least I had Jamie looking out for me, and making sure my ankle was okay. Without him, I wouldn't have made it to this cabin. I don't even want to imagine myself stuck out in the snowstorm, struggling to walk as I try to find shelter. Would I have even made it out there without freezing to death? He wouldn't let me do anything, wanting me to rest my ankle the best I could. Later Jamie had helped me move onto the couch with my feet up while he went to prepare something for dinner. He had found some mac and cheese, and cooked it. We sit on the couch eating it.

Later, he made us another hot chocolate.

"This is nice," I say.

"It is."

"Do you think the storm will stop by tomorrow?"

Jamie glances outside, the wind howling. "Who knows, but hopefully it does and we can get out of here."

A doubtful thought appears in my head that I shouldn't even think about. "What if we don't get out of here?"

Jamie looks at me for a second. He then leans over to the table and places his mug there. He then turns to me, careful not to hurt my ankle. He takes my hand into his.

"Don't think like that, O'Connor. We are going to get out of here, okay? Tomorrow's Christmas, and we will be able to leave, head back to the lodge and spend it with our families. I'm sure by tomorrow morning the snow will stop falling, okay?"

I nod. Of course that's what is going to happen. How could I think we weren't going to be able to get out of here? The snow couldn't keep falling. Okay, so the storm could go on for a couple of days, but I'm sure it's not going to do that tonight. It was going to stop so we could get out of here. I wasn't going to spend more than a day trapped in a cabin with Jamie Jackson.

"Also, I think we should sleep out here in the living room beside the fireplace."

I look at him, my hands wrapped around the warm mug. "You mean like sleep on the floor?"

"You don't have to sleep on the floor. You can sleep here on the couch if you want. But you are welcome to sleep on the floor with me."

I wanted to laugh at this. He can't be serious about me snuggling up beside him on the floor beside the fireplace? Please, I rather freeze to death than sleep on the floor with him.

"Why do you want to sleep on the floor for?" I point to the bedroom. "There's a bed right there. It will be more comfortable than the floor."

"I know, but with the snowstorm outside, I think we should stay as close to the fire as we can. We don't want to freeze."

Jamie had a point. If we wanted to get out of here alive, we needed to keep warm. Even if we hated each other's guts, without each other we may not survive.

Jamie grabs pillows and the quilt from the bedroom. I watch him as I sip my drink, spreading the quilt on the floor. He put the pillows on top of the blanket.

"Do you have a warm blanket?" I ask him.

"No. I couldn't find any more. So I might roll myself up in the quilt, like a sleeping bag."

I shake my head. As much as I hated this jerk, I wasn't going to let him freeze. I drink the last of my drink, then place my mug next to Jamie's on the coffee table. I then stood up, wincing, and limp over to Jamie, pulling the blanket off me.

"Here, take this," I say.

Jamie shakes his head. "You will freeze on the couch, O'Connor."

"No, I'm not."

Jamie stares at me for what feels like a long time before he takes the blanket from me. "Are you going to sleep on the floor with me?"

My arm freezes half way as I was putting it back to my side when he said this. Me? Sleeping on the floor with Jamie Jackson, the one person I much rather avoid and not be reminded that I'm spending the night with him in a cabin in the middle of nowhere until this snowstorm passes? That whole thought terrifies me.

I frown at him, coming to my senses and putting my arm at my side. "If this is some sick joke trying to get me to sleep with you, the answer is no. I'm going to sleep on the couch."

I turn to walk back to the couch when he speaks.

"I'm not the kind of guy who you think I am, Candice," he says. I turn to look at him. "I'm not doing this because I want to sleep with you. I'm not even thinking about that right now. I'm trying to make sure we are both warm enough so we don't get hypothermia. Yeah, we have the fire going, but the closer we are together, our body heat will keep each other warm."

As much as I wanted to believe Jamie that he wasn't trying to come onto me, I knew he was right about the storm and our chances of getting hypothermia if we didn't keep ourselves warm enough. I step forward and sit down on the quilt. Carefully not to hurt my ankle, I hug my legs, keeping my eyes on the fire than at Jamie.

He set the pillows behind us, and then grabs the warm blanket. He sits down beside me and spreads out the blanket around the both of us. Without a word, we stare at the fire in silence.

"I heard a rumor at school once," I say, my eyes still on the fire. From the corner of my eye, I see him look my way. "The rumor was you're a player, and you use girls for one thing only. You date them for a short time and then you toss them when you get what you want." I force myself to look at him. "That's why I thought you were trying to sleep with me."

Jamie shakes his head. "The rumor is untrue. I don't use girls and I'm not a player. I have had only two girlfriends. Chelsea Chamberlain was one of my girlfriends, but we broke up just after homecoming. Apparently, she used me to win Homecoming Queen. I also dated Stacey Miller for almost a year until she moved away. We tried to keep in contact, but long-distance didn't work for us. Stacey was my longest relationship. Chelsea and I were together for four months. Yes, I have dated other girls from school too, but that's all they were. Just dates. I went on one or two dates with a girl, maybe asked them to a dance, but I never felt anything towards them long enough to be in a relationship with them. I didn't sleep with them either."

I search his eyes to see if he was telling the truth, but I couldn't see any ticks to tell me he was lying.

"Okay," I answer. "If you say so."

I turn back to the fire.

"The rumor might be there because apparently my brother was a player when he was in school. So people probably just assumed I was also a player like him. But I'm not. And honestly, the only girl I ever slept with was Chelsea." He turns away, looking down at the blanket. "But if I had known she was only using me to win Homecoming Queen this year, I wouldn't even have dated her."

I look back at him, this sad look on his face, something I have never seen in him before. I have always known him to be this perfect guy that everyone worshipped, the star of the ice hockey team, charming and good looking. Except underneath all of that, he was struggling to be noticed by his family, and some girl he dated spread a rumor about him that wasn't true. For what? To gain popularity or something to make themselves look good by making Jamie look like the bad guy?

"I'm sorry if I believed any of those rumors," I answer.

He gives me a small smile. "It's okay. It's not your fault."

We hold our gaze for what felt like a long time before I turn away first, focusing on the flames.

"We should get some sleep," he says, as he gets up to walk over to the light switch.

He turns it off. The fire from the fireplace and lights from the Christmas tree giving us all the light we needed. He throws some more wood into the fire before sitting back down next to me.

We lie down on the floor, the blanket wrapped around us. I make sure no parts of my body are touching Jamie, keeping my ankle straight. We lie there in silence, listening to the cracking of the fire and the howling of the wind outside. I pray silently to myself that the snow will stop falling and we will be able to get out of here tomorrow.

\* \* \*

"Candice, wake up."

I open my eyes to Jamie shaking me gently. I groan and try to hide my head back under the pillow, my body is not ready to wake up, but he only grabs the pillow and moves it away from me.

I sit up, frowning at him. "What is your problem, Jamie?"

He gives me a serious look. "We have a problem, Candice. The storm has stopped, but we are snowbound."

# Chapter Fourteen

Snowbound. Trapped inside this cabin with Jamie Jackson for another day is not what I wanted. That was not the plan at all when I tried to get rid of him.

It had to be some kind of joke. We are not snowbound at all. He is making all of this up.

"No, we can't be." I kick off the blanket and get up, completely forgetting about my ankle, a sharp pain throbs as I move quickly.

"We are," Jamie confirms.

I limp over to the door and swing it open. On the other side is snow blocking the way out. I have no idea how deep the snow was, but it covered the whole doorway.

"No, no, no!"

I start to dig my way out, but Jamie grabs me around the waist and pulls me away from the door, closing it behind us.

I hit his arms. "Let me go!"

"We can't get out, Candice," Jamie tells me. He sets me

down near the blankets. "The snow is too deep. I have even tried the windows. We are trapped."

Panic rushes over me. Trapped. Trapped in the middle of nowhere in a cabin, snowbound. I'm trapped in here with the guy I hated. And no one knows where we are because I was being stupid, thinking it was smart to lead Jamie out here in hope he gets lost so he can't find his way back to the resort, and I could enjoy the rest of my vacation without worrying about him. But here I am, falling victim of my own karma that was meant for someone else. And now who knows what will happen all because of my stupid decision.

And out of all the days to be trapped in here with him, it has to be on Christmas Day!

I grab my phone that I had set on the table last night. My phone still displayed no signal.

"There's no signal on my phone!" I say, turning to Jamie with wide eyes. "How are we going to get out of here if we can't get a message out to anyone?"

Jamie takes a step towards me. "Everything is going to be okay, Candice. We are going to get out of here. I don't know how, but we will."

Tears prick at my eyelids. "How can everything be okay when we are trapped here? No one knows we are here."

"I'm sure the people who live here will come back soon."

"What if they don't?"

"They will, Candice. They will."

I sink to my knees, crying. "This is all my fault. I'm the one who got us into this mess."

Jamie comes to my side and pulls me into his arms. I rest my head on his shoulder as I cry.

"I'm so sorry, Jamie. I shouldn't have led you out here."

Jamie rubs a hand up and down my back.

"It's okay, Candice. We will find a way out of this. I'm sure there is going to be a search party for us, and as long as we keep the fire burning, someone might be able to see the smoke."

"But what if no one sees it?"

Jamie pulls away from me, and cups his hands on my jaw. He gently lifts my head to make me face him. As soon as my eyes meet his, something happens when I see how gentle and caring his eyes were, like he actually is concerned about me. My heart flips in my chest.

He gently strokes his thumb against my left cheek. "Listen to me, Candice. Everything is going to be alright. We will get out of here. Someone will find us."

"It's Christmas Day, Jamie. We should be with our families. They will be devastated that something terrible has happened to us. It's all my fault we are even out here."

"Stop blaming yourself, Candice. Look, okay so it's not the Christmas we planned to have with our families. But we are here with each other. That is better than being stranded outside in the freezing cold. We can get through this together. I can't tell you how long we are going to be in this cabin for. But hopefully it's only going to be a couple of days. When the people who lives here comes back, they will be able to help us."

I nod, knowing that everything he was saying was true. I just wish we didn't have to wait for so long to be rescued. I don't know how long I can go with being alone in here with Jamie.

"What are we going to do for the mean time until then?" I ask.

"Well, there is one thing we can do right now and that's eat something for breakfast. Are you hungry?" I nod. Jamie lets go of my face. "How about you go and freshen up, and I will make breakfast?"

I agree to the idea. Jamie helps me to my feet.

"You will be alright in the shower?"

I nod. "I will be fine."

"Okay. Call out if you need me."

Jamie disappears to the kitchen to cook, while I limp to the bathroom to take a shower. I check my ankle while I was in there. The swelling had gone down, but the bruising was still there. I make the shower quick because I couldn't stand on my ankle for too long. As I get dress back into my clothes, I smell pancakes coming from the kitchen.

I limp to the kitchen where Jamie is putting on the final touches for breakfast. He sets two plates down on the two seated table. Two glasses of orange juice were already on the table, along with a bottle of maple syrup. He gestures for me to sit down.

I sit down, inhaling the pancake scent, which made my stomach grumble.

Jamie sits across from me.

"I love pancakes," I say, reaching for my glass of orange juice. "Did you make these from scratch?" I take a sip of my drink.

Jamie shakes his head, reaching across the table for the syrup. "No. I found a pancake mix in the pantry." He squirts the syrup over his pancakes before passing the bottle towards me.

I put my glass down, thanking him, and grab the bottle. I pour it on top of my pancakes. "Thank you for breakfast, Jamie."

Jamie smiles. "No worries, O'Connor."

We dig into the food in silence, enjoying every moment of it.

After breakfast I offer to help Jamie clean up, but he wants me to sit and rest my ankle.

"How is your ankle this morning?" he asks me, turning the tap on.

"The swelling has gone down," I answer. "There's a bruise."

"When I finish cleaning up, I will bandage your ankle, okay?"

I nod. "Okay."

I get up and decide to sit down beside the Christmas tree. Although my family wasn't doing presents this year, if I was back at the lodge, my family and I would be getting up to head to the dining room for breakfast. Later we will spend the day in town at the Christmas market.

Now, because of my disappearance, I'm sure they wouldn't be going to the Christmas market. My parents would be staying close to the lodge, hoping I would show up.

Jamie joins me a few minutes later, a bandage in his hand.

"Can I have a look at your ankle?" he asks.

I nod, and he gently places my foot on his lap. His hands are warm as he examines my ankle.

"Does it still hurt?" he asks.

"Only if I move too fast."

"Okay, well try to keep your foot up today." He begins to wrap the bandage around. When it's done, he looks up me. "It's not too tight?"

I shake my head. "No, it's fine."

He let's go of my foot, gently putting it back down on the floor. He turns to look at the tree, silence growing between us. With us being stuck in here for who knows how long, I wonder what we are going to do in here. We couldn't just sit here in silence until we are rescued.

"So what are we going to do until we can get out of here?" I ask.

Jamie turns to me, shrugging. "I don't know." He looks around the cabin. "Honestly this place doesn't look like there is much for us to do."

"Maybe we could find a game board or something and play that to pass the time?"

Jamie nods. "I will look around."

He gets up, but before he walks away, he looks down at me. "Actually, there is something I thought we could do. I was thinking about it while I was cooking breakfast. I thought it might cheer you up a bit, but I'm not sure if you can do it with your sprain ankle."

"What is it?"

Jamie walks over to a radio that's on a table beside the bookshelf. He switches it on and an upbeat Christmas song is playing.

"Are you suggesting we sing karaoke or something?" I ask. "I will warn you. I'm not a great singer."

He walks back over to me. "Actually, I thought we could dance."

I stare at him. "Dance?"

He nods. "Yeah, I thought dancing will cheer you up a bit. But I understand if you don't want to because of your ankle. We don't have to go all out with fast dance moves, but I thought because of your ankle we could do a slow dance."

A slow dance. Jamie Jackson wanted to slow dance with me. A million things ran through my head, and I can just imagine what Gabriella will say if she was here right now. But it doesn't mean anything, right? He is only choosing to slow dance with me because of my ankle so we aren't going so fast that would hurt my ankle more.

"I thought you said I need to keep my ankle up," I answer.

"I know I said that. It's just that there isn't much stuff we can do in here to past the time. If there was a television, we would sit down and watch something. You know what? You're right. We shouldn't dance. You should rest your ankle instead. It was a stupid thing to ask you."

He switches off the radio, and I almost feel bad that he had asked me to dance. But I'm glad he made the call not to because I really didn't want to dance with him. Not because of my sprained ankle, but in general. We are enemies. We don't dance together. Even if we are trapped in this cabin, it doesn't mean we are friends at all. Maybe we had to get along in here to survive, but as soon as we get out of here, we will go back to hating each other.

Yet, seeing the disappointed look in his face crushes my heart. He had thought this could have been a fun activity for us to do, but my ankle wasn't going to let me do anything.

"Let's dance later tonight," I say.

Jamie turns to me. "Tonight?"

I nod, smiling. "Yeah, I think it would be good to do it tonight. We could do it after dinner. Like you said, I should really keep my ankle up today. If I do that, maybe it won't hurt so much when we go to dance."

Jamie smiles. "Yeah, definitely. I think tonight will be perfect. Especially if we turn off the lights, and have the glow from the fire and the Christmas tree lights."

I imagine this in my head and it really sounded magical. "I like that."

"I will go slow. I promise. I don't want you to hurt your ankle more."

All I do is nod, because suddenly everything just seems strange between us. We weren't fighting. We were talking about doing things together. Things that sounded romantic. The thought of it made me sick to the stomach. I didn't want to do anything romantic with Jamie, and I'm sure he doesn't want to do anything romantic with me either.

"Okay, so dancing aside," Jamie breaks the silence first. "Do you still want to play a game? Or should we give that karaoke idea you had a go?"

I raise my eyebrows at him. "My idea? I never suggested it."

"Sure you did. You thought that's what I was planning to do."

"Which you aren't, and I'm not singing in front of you."

"Right, but you sang in front of strangers the other night, so what's the difference between me and those strangers?"

He had a point, but I really wasn't in a singing mood right now. "Maybe it's something we can do later. I want to do something other than dancing and singing."

"Okay, well let me go and find a board game." He stands up.

I look around the room, wondering what the two of us could do to past the time. Something that didn't involve romantic activities.

My eyes land on the bookshelf. "Actually, how about you pick a book from the shelf and read it to me?"

Jamie follows my gaze towards the bookshelf. He turns to look back at me. "Are you sure you want me to do that?"

I nod. "I'm sure. If that's okay with you."

"I don't mind."

He walks over to the bookshelf and browses the books. He picks out a brown hardcover book and turns the cover around for me to see. "There's mostly classics on the shelf. What do you think of *Journey to the Centre of the Earth* by Jules Verne?"

"Yeah, sure," I say. "I have seen the movies, but I haven't read the book yet."

"Sweet." He walks over to me. "I had this book on my summer reading list once. I loved it."

I raise my eyebrow. "I didn't think you were the reading type."

He stands next to the couch. "I mostly read for English, but sometimes I like to sit down with a good book that I don't have to read for class." He gestures to the couch. "Why don't you sit up here, O'Connor? It will be more comfortable on the couch."

I nod, getting off the floor and take a seat on the couch. I put my ankle up and then Jamie sits at the other end.

He opens the book and begins reading. His voice is gentle as he reads, and it was like listening to an audiobook. I listen carefully to the story, the cracking of the fire making it sound perfect. Maybe Christmas or my plan to get rid of Jamie didn't work out the way I had planned, but sitting on the couch with him as he reads was a good enough way for me to spend Christmas.

# Chapter Fifteen

I lost count of how long Jamie had read the book, but somehow during his reading I had gotten comfy and fallen asleep. When I wake up, my head is resting against his shoulder. Jamie is also asleep, the book sitting on the armrest.

I rub my eyes, carefully sitting up so I didn't wake Jamie. He doesn't stir. I watch him as he sleeps peacefully. Watching him sleep made me want to curl back up on the couch and fall asleep beside him, and stay there until we can get out of here. I wonder what he must be dreaming about. Maybe he was dreaming about what he could be doing with his family. I know I did just a few minutes ago before I woke up.

But I wasn't dreaming about spending Christmas back at the lodge with my family. I was dreaming about being back at home where my grandparents are with us, along with other members of my family. Belle was walking around with a fluffy red and white collar, along with a Santa hat. It was Hannah's idea to dress her up like that, and you can full on see it in

Belle's face how much she hated it. The whole house smells delicious with the ham and roast vegetables

And then all of that disappeared when I woke up, reminding me of how stupid I was.

Leaving Jamie to sleep, I get up and walk over to the fireplace, adding more logs. I then limp to the kitchen, feeling like another hot chocolate. I make one for Jamie too, setting it down on the table. As I'm sitting back down on the couch, Jamie wakes up.

He rubs his eyes looking over at me. "Hey."

I give him a small smile as I wrap my hands around the warm mug, sitting back on the couch. "Hey. I made you a hot chocolate."

He looks over at the streamy mug. "Thanks."

He leans across to grab it and sits back. "What time is it?" He takes a sip of his hot chocolate.

I shrug. "I don't know." There wasn't a clock in here. It was like whoever lived here just wanted to lock themselves away from the rest of the world.

"I didn't realize I had fallen asleep. I saw you fall asleep, so I put the book down, and I must have dosed off."

"Well, maybe if we sleep, time will go by quicker."

"True." He takes a sip. "Are you hungry? I can make something to eat. Would you like some grilled cheese again?"

"Grilled cheese will be great."

Jamie drinks more of the hot chocolate. I watch him as he sips it. For a moment I wondered what it would be like if I could kiss him. But then I remind myself how much I hate him. Seriously, but where did that thought even come from? He doesn't notice me watching him though. He places his mug on the table and gets up, telling me he will be back soon.

All I do is nod. I was afraid to say something. This morning I already felt weird. First, Jamie and I weren't fighting, and then I wondered what it would be like to kiss him. Seriously, what is wrong with me?

Maybe I have a case of cabin fever. Is that a thing?

While he makes us something to eat, I keep sipping my drink. I tell myself to think about something else other than Jamie. Maybe it will stop these strange things I'm feeling. So I decided to think about the winter dance instead. I thought of what we could do for the decorations, but my mind was blank.

"What are you thinking about?"

I look up to see Jamie standing next to me. I put my mug down and grab the plate.

"Just thinking about the winter dance," I answer. "That's all."

"Have you come up with any ideas for decorations yet?" he asks, sitting down beside me. He takes a huge bite of his grilled cheese.

I shake my head. "No, not yet. What about you?"

He shakes his head and swallows his food. "No, nothing yet either. I will probably brainstorm ideas before we go back to school."

"Yeah, same here."

I bite into my sandwich and chew it slowly.

"Are you excited for the dance?" he asks me.

I nod, turning to him as I swallow. "Of course. Dances are exciting. It's also our last school dance before prom, and I can't wait to make the most of it."

Jamie nods, smiling. "Definitely true. I know it's too early to ask this, but are you planning to go with anyone?"

I stop my sandwich on its way to my mouth. I turn to

Jamie who was watching me carefully. Why would he ask me that? I shake my head. "No. There's no one I would like to go with. I think I'm just going to go with Allegra if no one asks her to the dance."

"I'm thinking of asking Chelsea to the dance."

I raise my eyebrow. "Chelsea Chamberlain?"

He nods.

"I thought you guys broke up?"

"We did, but we are still very good friends."

I sit back on the couch, resting my ankle up. "I don't think you should ask Chelsea."

Jamie looks at me. "Why not? Are you saying I shouldn't go with a friend?"

He eats the rest of the sandwich in his hand, the other one still sitting on his plate. How did he eat one so quickly and I hadn't even finished the first one I have bitten into yet?

I shake my head. "No. I'm not saying that. You can go with whoever you want. But I don't think Chelsea is going to want to go with you."

His shoulders sink with disappointment. "Why do you say that?"

Gosh, why am I giving him advice on who he should be going to the dance with when I don't even care who his date is? Honestly, I'd much rather if he didn't show up to the dance at all.

"Well, the way I see it, Chelsea is beautiful, and she knows it. And if she dated you once, only to win Homecoming Queen, then she is probably going to want to go to the dance with someone else. Not with you. And even though we don't win anything at the winter dance, she is going to go to it with someone she can stand out with to make sure everyone knows who she is, and who she is with. And from what I know about Chelsea is she has shown up to our school dances with a different date all the time. She is the kind of girl who gets bored easily with the same guy. She always wants to be on top, so she will keep looking for ways to stay on top even if it means dating different guys, using them only to get what she wants."

Jamie thinks about this for a second. "I never saw it like that. Well, maybe you and I should go to the dance with each other?"

He says this just as I bite into my sandwich, and I almost choke on my food. I start coughing. Jamie curses and gets up, putting his plate on the table and comes around me to pat me on the back. When I stopped coughing, I push Jamie's arm away from me.

"What are you trying to do?" I frown at him. "Are you trying to kill me?"

"How am I trying to kill you, O'Connor?"

"By suggesting we go to the dance together while I had food in my mouth."

Jamie gives me a confused look. "How was that my fault, O'Connor?"

"It just is, Jamie. Why would you even suggest that anyway?"

"What? That we should go to the dance together? Why do you think we shouldn't go to the dance together?"

I laugh. "Well, for one thing we are enemies, Jamie. Enemies don't go to dances together."

Now this is how I like it. Back to fighting instead of having those strange feelings towards him. Maybe I don't have cabin fever after all. We just had to find the right thing to fight about and we were back to our old selves again.

"Is that why you wouldn't dance with me earlier?" Jamie asks. "Not because of your ankle, but because we are enemies?"

I didn't answer him because I didn't know how to answer it. Yes, we are enemies and that was part of it. But it was the slow dancing part that really scared me. The very thought of doing something romantic with Jamie terrified me. It just didn't feel right to slow dance with him. Sure, he was thinking about my ankle and thought that dancing slow was better for me than dancing fast, but still we were doing something romantic. Maybe it didn't mean anything. Maybe it was to pass the time. Still, it was something I didn't think we should do.

"Fine," he says, taking his plate and walking away from the couch. "We won't dance. We won't do anything. We will just wait here, bored to death, while we wait for someone to come rescue us."

He sits down next to the fire with his back to me.

I sit there, staring at my sandwich that I suddenly have no appetite for. Why do I feel bad for treating Jamie like this? One dance shouldn't hurt right? But what's the point dancing together if we are enemies? Yeah, we could be nice with each other while we are stuck in here, but what will happen once we get out of here?

*One dance, Candice*, I say to myself. *That's all you have to do with him.*

Putting my plate on the table next to my mug, I get up and limp over to the radio. I switch it on and an upbeat Christmas song comes on. I look over at Jamie, who has turned to look at me.

"So you want to dance?" I say. "Okay, let's dance."

Jamie stands up, but doesn't make his way over to me. "Are you sure, Candice? We don't have to. You can keep resting your ankle, and we can do this later."

I roll my eyes. "Get over here, Jamie, before I change my mind. You just complained to me that I didn't want to dance with you because we are enemies. Yes, we are enemies. And once we get out of here, we are never even going to be doing this again. So let's just have this one dance."

Jamie's lips curl into a smirk. He puts his plate on the coffee table and walks over to me. We don't take our eyes off each other as he makes his way over to me. The song that is playing finishes, and a slow Christmas song comes on. I don't know which song it was. I haven't heard of this one before, and I'm already hating it. I can feel my brain exploding from the irritation. Up-beat Christmas songs are what I like the most. But even though this song was terrible, it was perfect for our slow dance. It was like this radio station knew what we were doing and had put it on for us.

Jamie takes my hand, putting his other hand on my lower back, pulling me closer to him, and then rests it on my hip. I put my free hand on his shoulder.

"We will go as slow as we can," he says. "Let me know if your ankle starts to hurt, and we will stop."

I nod. "Okay."

We start swaying to the music, our eyes never leaving each other. My heart pounds a million miles per hour against my rib cage. I can't believe I'm actually dancing with Jamie. Never in a million years would I have thought I would even stand this close to him.

We move slowly across the room. We step to the left and then to the right, one step backward then forward repeatedly thought the whole dance. He doesn't spin or dips me, maybe it was because of my ankle. Worrying about my ankle through this dance had been for nothing, because the slow movements didn't put too much pressure on my ankle. It hurt a little when I turn, but I was busy concentrating on him instead of my ankle. As much as I don't want to admit this, it felt nice to be doing this. Why had I been so worried about dancing with him even if we are enemies?

The song comes to an end, but we don't move from each other straight away. My eyes drifts to his lips for a brief second before I look back at his eyes. I notice him looking at my own lips. He starts to lean forward, and I feel myself panicking. Was Jamie Jackson actually going to kiss me?

But before he did anything I didn't want him to do, he steps backwards, letting go of my hand and dropping his hand from my waist.

"Thanks for the dance," he says.

I nod. "Yeah. Thanks."

Jamie moves to turn off the radio, sending the cabin into silence. I continue standing there, keeping my eyes on the floor as Jamie moves over to the table, grabbing his plate and heads towards the kitchen.

What had just happened between us?

# Chapter Sixteen

I'm imagining things. Nothing happened between Jamie and me. That dance meant nothing, and we didn't feel anything. So why did it feel awkward all of a sudden? We haven't even said anything to each other since we ended the dance and finished our lunch.

But of course we can't avoid each other for long in this tiny cabin.

We were back sitting on the couch later after Jamie clear up the dishes. The first thing he says to break the silence between us is ask me how my ankle was. I answer it was fine. It did hurt a little while I was dancing, but with the slow movements, it didn't throb as much.

We are back to being silent again, watching the fire. The cracking of the fire fills the silence between us.

When I can't stand the silence any longer, I break it. "Let's play a game."

Jamie snaps himself out of his thoughts and turns to me.

"What kind of game do you want to play?"

"Let's not play a board game. I was thinking of playing something like 20 Questions."

It wasn't exactly a game I wanted to play with Jamie. He wasn't exactly someone I wanted to get to know, but it was the first thing that came to my head. It's definitely a game we could play to past the time.

Jamie nods. "Sure. I would love to play. Do you want to go first?"

I think of a question. "If you didn't have to come out to Rocky Springs Ski Resort with your parents, what would you be doing for winter break instead?"

Jamie rubs a hand over his chin to think. "I would probably hang out with my friends. We may not be able to go to the skating rink to play hockey, but we would probably play it in the driveway at someone's house to get some practice in before school starts again."

I raise my eyebrows. "Hockey? Do you do anything else other than play hockey?"

"It's my favorite sport." He shrugs. "I also believe that's two questions you asked me. Aren't you supposed to ask one question and then I ask you a question after I answer mine?"

I roll my eyes. "Don't tell me you are the kind of person who sticks to the rules when playing a game."

"What's wrong with that?"

I shrug. "Nothing. I never really took you as the kind of person to follow rules."

Jamie raises his eyebrows. "What makes you think I don't follow rules?"

"Well for one thing, people worship you at school. I kind of figured you are the kind of person to get away with everything."

"I hate to break it to you, O'Connor, but I don't get away with everything."

I wanted to argue this with him, not wanting to believe that any of this is true. He's a jock. Jocks get away with everything at our school.

"Okay, okay, whatever," I answer. "So what's your question for me?"

"Do you know what you would like to do after high school?"

"I plan to go to college and study journalism."

"Interesting. That's great you know what you are going to do. I still don't know what I want to study or go after high school. All I know is I want to play ice hockey in college."

"Nice. Okay, so now I can ask you this question. Do you do anything else other than play hockey?"

"Of course I do, O'Connor. Why do you assume I play hockey all the time? I do take time out to do other stuff like hang out with family and friends."

"Fair enough. Okay, your turn. Ask away."

We went back and forth, asking each other questions. It's not until the fifteenth question where we started to get more personal.

"Why don't your family come to see you at your games?" I ask. "I have seen Estelle at a few of them."

Jamie doesn't answer me straight away. "Well, Estelle doesn't come to anymore now that she moved to France. I don't really know why. My parents used to come for Edward's games and to see Estelle cheer, but for whatever reason they have gotten too busy to come see me."

I was really surprised to hear about this. It wasn't

something I expected about the Jackson family. I don't know so much about Jamie's brother, but I started high school when he was in twelfth grade. I remember watching some games Edward Jackson had played in, and seeing his parents come watch. Estelle was the oldest out of her brothers, so I never saw her at any games, but I have heard a lot about her from other students. After Edward graduated, I had seen Estelle come to the games instead of her parents for Jamie's games. For the past year I hadn't seen her, and now I know it's because she had moved to France.

"What made you really hate me?" Jamie suddenly asks me when I stay quiet about his answer. I really didn't know what to say about his previous answer. Or maybe he just wanted to quickly move on before I even had a chance to respond when I thought about what he had said. "And I don't mean about snatching the pencil from you."

I think about this one. When did I came to realize how much I hated him?

"I don't remember. All I know is that besides the pencil, you would make fun of my hair. Over time you did things to irritate me, and I guess that grew into hatred."

Jamie nods slowly. "I'm really sorry for ever making fun of your hair. The hair color is beautiful. Forget everything I had ever said about it."

"I can never forget what you say about me, but I forgive you."

Jamie gives me a small smile. "Thanks, O'Connor."

"Since we are on this subject, why did you act so rude and snatched the pencil from me? Out of everyone at our table, why did you choose me? Like, there was two pencil tins for everyone at our table to share. I'm sure there was another dark blue pencil you could have used, but you took mine before I could even finish coloring."

"Wow. You can still remember the exact color of the pencil?" He chuckles. "I honestly don't remember what color it was. All I remember is snatching it right out of your hand so I could use it."

"Yeah, it's something I keep playing over and over in my head whenever I see you. So, Jamie, why did you take it? Why didn't you snatch it from someone else?"

"Okay, one question at a time, O'Connor. That's the whole point of the game. One question at a time."

I roll my eyes. "Whatever. Just answer the question."

"I actually don't remember, O'Connor. You're talking about something that happened almost twelve years ago. All I know is that I was a little brat when I was six. I snatched the pencil from you because you were the closest to me. Also, I didn't exactly had manners then and never really asked or say thank you when I wanted something. I just did it without asking."

I shake my head. "That still doesn't give you the right to do what you did. I didn't understand why you had done it, and never snatched any pencils from the other kids. Right after that is when you began teasing me."

"I know, and I'm sorry that I did. I'm not pleased with myself for what I have done to you over the years. Truth be told, O'Connor, I never intended to tease you. When you got upset over the pencil, I didn't realize it had upset you. And when I asked you why your hair was red, I didn't know at the time that it was rude to ask someone that. I'm sorry if I had offended you on that. I know from time to time I may throw jokes in about your hair color, and I know it's something I shouldn't do. But there was something about the way you would get upset over the littlest things that made me want to keep teasing you, just to see you get upset."

He thought teasing me was a fun way to upset me?

I frown. "Seriously? You thought it would be funny?"

"Like I said. I was a bit of a brat back then."

"Who cares if you were a brat back then? You could have stopped teasing me over time, but you didn't! You kept going and never cared how I felt about it."

"I'm sorry, O'Connor."

I stood up from the couch too fast, and a sharp pain shot up through my ankle. I wince.

Jamie gets up, looking at me with real concern. After everything I had said to him, is he really concern for me? Or does he want to make me think he cares? I bet when we return to school after break, no doubt he will be making fun of me to all his friends. He will tell them all about what I had tried to do, and how we both got snowbound in this cabin. I wouldn't be surprised if he spreads lies about everything we do in here.

"Candice."

I held up my arms in defence. "No. Don't act all concerned about me. Just do me a favor and stay away from me."

"How am I going to stay away from you when we are trapped in this cabin until someone comes to dig us out of here?"

I put my arms at my side. "I don't know. I just don't want you near me. Not if you think upsetting me is amusing to you."

"I'm sorry, O'Connor."

"Will you stop apologizing? And can you *please* stop calling me by my surname. My name is Candice. Call me Candice. Not O'Connor. You can apologize all you want, but it's never going to make me stop hating you, Jamie Jackson."

He opens his mouth to say something, but then closes it. We stand there, staring at each other until finally I break eye contact. I turn and limp to the bedroom, closing the door. There was no lock, and there wasn't anything I could put up against the door knob. I stand there staring at the knob, waiting for Jamie to come in and argue with me.

It doesn't take long for him to be at the door, knocking, begging me to open up and let him in. I lean my back up against the door and put all of my weight against it so it can't be opened.

"Candice, please open up. Let us talk. Look, we may never have gotten along with each other in the past, but we can change now."

Change? He thinks we can change now? All because we are in this cabin together? Yeah, I don't think anything is ever going to change between us. We are always going to be enemies no matter what.

When he realizes I wasn't going to open the door, he stops knocking. It's quiet on the other side. I stay by the door for a few more minutes before I sit down on the bed. I was better off in here, away from Jamie where I couldn't be irritated by him. I will stay here until we are rescued.

But I can't help think about the dance we had done. What had happened between us since then and now? When we were dancing, it was like we had chemistry that we never really knew we had. Then as soon as we started asking personal questions during twenty questions, that chemistry faded. We were back to our old selves.

Yet, I can't help to feel bummed about it all. I shouldn't feel like this when I hate him, right?

# Chapter Seventeen

Staying hidden in the bedroom was impossible when it was just the two of us in here. I knew eventually I had to come out here if I wanted to use the bathroom or if I wanted some food to eat. The main objection was to keep warm. It was cold in the bedroom, there wasn't a heater in here.

It didn't help that Jamie was cooking. The smell of steak fills the whole cabin. It made my stomach grumble no matter how hard I tried not to think about food. So after spending a few hours alone in the bedroom, I walked out.

I didn't head to the kitchen. Instead, I sit down on the couch, watching the fire. I grab the blanket on the couch and wrap it around me.

The floorboards creak behind me and I turn to see Jamie walking back into the living room with two plates. He stops short when he sees me.

"Oh. You came out," he says.

"Yeah, it was cold and the smell of food was making my

stomach grumble. What's for dinner?"

Jamie walks towards me. "I warmed up the leftover mac and cheese. I also found some steak in the freezer, so I cooked it up. I was going to serve it with salad too, but there wasn't any lettuce in the fridge."

"That's fine, Jamie." He hands me my plate. "Thank you."

He sits down next to me and we eat in silence. Jamie doesn't say anything to me until we finish eating. He gets up and takes our plates. He glances outside for a brief second before turning back to me.

"It's getting dark," he says. "What do you want to do tonight?"

I shrug. "I don't know."

"Would you like a hot chocolate?"

"Yes please."

Jamie leaves to the kitchen to wash up. He puts on the kettle to make the hot chocolate.

While he does that, I go over to the window and look through. There was nothing to see beside the snow all piled up around the cabin. I sigh. It seemed almost impossible to get out of here, and who knew how long it would take anyone to dig us out. I wonder if the person who lives here will be back soon.

"Everything okay, Candice?"

I turn to face Jamie. I had no idea how long I had been staring out of the window, but I hadn't heard him returning. He has two steamy mugs of hot chocolate in his hands.

I nod. "Yeah. Just wondering how long the snow will be like this before someone comes and digs us out. Or if the people who live here will return any time soon."

"I'm sure everything is going to turn out fine, Candice."

He nods towards the fireplace. "Come on. Let's sit beside the fireplace."

I listen to him and sit down on the quilt. Jamie sits down beside me, handing me my mug before wrapping himself with the blanket also.

We sit sipping our drinks as we stare at the fire, not daring to speak in case it lead to another argument. And it will because that's how we are. We were sworn enemies from that day one in kindergarten that started our conflict. Even when we graduate in six months and disappear to different colleges where we will finally be away from each other, we probably would not survive at our high school reunion in the future. I can just imagine us showing up to the reunion with our future partners, and all we will do is bicker the whole night.

"Candice, please don't be mad with me, but I am truly sorry about everything over the years," he says. I keep my eyes on my hot chocolate. Looking at him will make me angry. "I know snatching that pencil away from you didn't give me the right to act the way I did over the years towards you. I know that once we get out of this cabin, we will go back to the way we have always been at school. We won't talk to each other, and we probably won't get this close again. Please forgive me, Candice. I promise I won't tease you ever again."

I let his words sink into me, then I force myself to look at him. His eyes plead with me to forgive him. I don't know if I want to ever forgive him. I don't even want to talk or be near him again once we get out of here. I was seriously done with Jamie Jackson. I just wanted to get through the rest of the school year without him causing trouble for me. And I seriously doubt he will stick to his promise. He will never be done causing trouble for me.

"If you can prove to me that you won't tease me, I will forgive you," I answer. "But if you can't, then I will never forgive you."

Jamie nods. "Of course. I totally understand. Starting right now, I'm not going to tease you. Ever. I promise. If I break that promise, you have the right to do whatever you want to me."

We continue to stare at each other as we come to this agreement. A few minutes passed, and we are still staring. I stare at his lips, but I quickly forced myself to look away. I couldn't think that way towards him.

He wraps an arm around me and pulls me close to him. I can feel his body heat against mine, and it was causing all kinds of mixed feelings, ones I shouldn't even be feeling towards Jamie. We were enemies for a reason. It would be weird to feel something towards him, right?

I rest my head against his shoulder. "What happens if we are stuck in here forever?"

Jamie chuckles. "We won't be stuck here forever, O'Connor. Snow melts, you know?"

"I know it does. But we could get another really bad storm and be snowbound in here again."

"You worry too much, O'Connor."

I lift my head up and face him. "I do not."

"You do." Jamie puts his mug down. With his arm still around me, his other hand brushes my cheek as he tucks a strand of my hair behind my ear. A shiver runs down my spine from his touch. What is this guy doing to me? "No one may not have found us today. But we don't know what tomorrow will bring us."

I nod, knowing he was right. "I hope so. I can't stand to worry my parents another day."

The arm he had wrapped around my shoulders moves to

my back, where he rubs his hand up and down to soothe me. As he does, there's this weird feeling in the pit of my stomach. Butterflies, maybe? I don't know, but it shouldn't even be there.

"I'm the same with my parents too," he says. "Everything will be okay. We have each other."

"I don't know what I would do if we had to stay here longer."

Jamie's lips curl into a smirk, dropping his arms. "Why? Because you have to be stuck in this cabin with me? Gee, O'Connor, every girl at school would want to be in your position right now."

"Jamie, you are so full of yourself."

He scoffs. "I'm full of myself, am I? Tell me, why is that?"

I shrug. "You just are. You have this perfect charm and you always expect people to like you."

Jamie raises an eyebrow. "I have a perfect charm and everyone likes me, huh?"

"Yes."

"Well, shouldn't you like me too then?"

I stare at him. Was he seriously asking me that question?

"I can never like you."

"Why not?"

Why was he asking me this? He should know the history we have between us that makes us not able to ever like each other. It was just impossible for us. Not with the constant fighting we have between each other.

"Look at everything that happened between us over the years," I point out. "How can we like each other when we constantly fight?"

"People can change."

"I doubt you and I will ever change the way we feel about each other. There's too much conflict between us."

I wait for Jamie to respond back, but he doesn't. Instead, he reaches up and touches the side of my cheek, resting it there. With his thumb, he strokes the corner of my mouth, and I hold my breath for a second. What was he doing?

We stay that way for a few minutes until he finally drops his hand and I let go of the breath I had been holding.

What just happened?

"We should get some sleep, Jamie," I say, drinking the last of my hot chocolate. "I'm a little tired."

"Right, yeah, okay." He drinks the rest of his hot chocolate and place the mug on the table. He takes mine and place it next to his. "Good night, O'Connor."

"Good night, Jamie."

\* \* \*

I wake up in the middle of the night to find myself snuggling up against Jamie's shoulder, my hand rested on his chest.

I move my hand from his chest and move an inch away from him. He doesn't stir in his sleep. I watch him for a second, trying to figure out what was happening between us. I hope we don't stay here for too long because I really do not like how this cabin is bringing us together, changing us. I can never like Jamie Jackson and I don't want to feel anything towards him. Even if I do develop a crush on him, I will only get my heart broken, and I didn't want that.

I rest my head back on my pillow and went back to sleep. As I close my eyes again, I think about what Jamie had said earlier: Can the two of us change our feelings? Will that explain the mixed feelings I have towards him at the moment?

# Chapter Eighteen

"Candice, wake up."

Jamie shakes me a couple of times until I groan and finally open my eyes. He is sitting beside me, his hand resting on my arm.

"What?" I ask him, still half asleep. I yawn. "What time is it?"

"It's around eight thirty," he answers. "Candice, I heard something outside."

I raise my eyebrows at him. He woke me up just to tell me he heard something outside? "Really, Jamie? You're waking me up because you heard a noise? I'm pretty sure you're old enough not to wake me over a scary noise you heard."

He gives me a dirty look. "Not that kind of noise, O'Connor. I heard something that sounded like an engine."

I bolted upright when he says this. "You're serious? You heard an engine?"

He nods.

"Like a rescue team?"

He shakes his head. "No, I don't think so. I think it's whoever lives here. They seemed to have gone away for Christmas, and now they are returning home."

I leap up from the floor, limping over to the window to see if I can spot anyone like Jamie had said. He follows behind me and we both peer out the window. It was still hard to see through the window with the snow up on the porch. But it only covered the bottom part of the window, where we were able to see an elderly man with a younger man shovelling the snow.

I can't believe it that we were finally getting out of here! At least we weren't trapped in here for more than a day, and these men will be able to help us to get back to the resort. Honestly, I don't think I can handle another day with Jamie in this cabin.

Jamie taps on the glass, hoping the two men will be able to hear it and look our way.

The young man looks up, looking around before glancing our way, surprised to see us. We wave to him so he knew we were trapped in here and needed to get out. The young man calls out to the elderly man, pointing to us. He looks our way, then says something to the young man. The two of them worked together in digging a path in the snow towards the door. It was going to take them a while to dig to the door, so Jamie sat me down on the couch. He had prepared breakfast for us while I was asleep and set the grilled cheese sandwiches on the table for us.

But the happy feeling inside of me to know that we are finally being rescued after being trapped in here for a day and a half, didn't allow me to have much of an appetite. I try not to think that I was going to get in huge trouble by my parents for sneaking away from the resort. All I try to do is remind myself that I was finally getting away from Jamie and I will see my family again.

Most likely, I would be grounded so it will mean staying in the hotel room as punishment. While I'm sad that I won't be able to enjoy the rest of the vacation, on the bright side, I won't have to see Jamie, and I can rest my ankle properly.

It's half an hour before the two men were able to dig to the front door. They open it, walk inside. Jamie and I stand up from the couch.

"What are you two doing inside my house?" the elderly man demanded. "Tell me one good reason why I shouldn't call the police right now to report you two for trespassing."

The younger man put a hand on the elderly man's shoulder. "Dad, I think that's the two teenagers who were on the news yesterday, missing from Rocky Springs Ski Resort."

Jamie nods. "Yes, that's us. We are so sorry to be inside your cabin. We had wandered off from the resort, and got caught in the snowstorm. We couldn't find our way back, stumbled upon your cabin, and took shelter here. We were only going to stay overnight until the storm passes, but when we woke up the next morning, we were snowed in."

The elderly man looks between us. "I see."

"We promise you that we were just seeking shelter from the storm, and not breaking in," I say.

"We ate some food." Jamie gestures to me. "Candice also sprained her ankle and I used a bandaged from your first aid kit."

The elderly man continues to look at us, and I thought that maybe he was going to tell us off for being in here. That he wasn't going to have the heart to care what the two of us have gone through, and we had no right to be in his house. I totally understood if he gets upset with us. We broke into his house without permission. Even if there wasn't a storm, we still seek shelter in here without consent when nobody was home.

But surprisingly he wasn't mad with us.

"It's good to see you kids are alright," he says. "Is there anything I can do for you?" He turns to me. "Is your ankle okay?"

I nod. "It's okay, just sore."

"We are pretty much fine," Jamie says. "The only thing you could do for us is help us to get back to Rocky Springs Ski Resort."

The elderly man nods. "Of course." He turns to his son. "Peter here can take you back there."

Jamie nods. "That will be great. Thank you so much."

"How long have you kids been in here?" Peter wants to know.

"We have been here since Friday afternoon when the snowstorm hit on Christmas Eve."

"You kids are very lucky my dad has a snowplow on the front of his truck," Peter tells us. "Otherwise you may be waiting for days or weeks until his driveway is plowed. The council wouldn't think about plowing to clear this driveway, as it's private use."

I couldn't imagine being in here alone with Jamie for days, maybe weeks, just to wait until we were rescued from the snow. I'm grateful that I don't have to be here another moment longer. I'm sure one of us would end up killing the other by then. I will be able to reunite with my family soon. I can just imagine Gabriella asking me all sorts of questions about Jamie, but she wasn't getting any answers at all. There isn't anything to tell about what went on between Jamie and I while we were alone in here. Nothing anyone needed to know.

I mean, no one needs to know about the strange mixed feelings I had felt towards him yesterday. They probably don't mean anything anyway.

At least I don't think they do.

"Dad, I will be back soon." Peter turns to Jamie and I. "Are you kids ready to go?"

\* \* \*

Jamie and I sat in the front seat of the truck that belonged to the elderly man. I sat in the middle while Peter sat at the wheel. The rental snowboards were strapped in the back of the pick-up truck. He drives carefully down the long and windy driveway. I wonder how far away the main road is.

"Thank you very much for driving us back to the resort," Jamie says.

"It's no problem at all," Peter says. "At least my father's cabin was a safe haven for you two during the storm. He built it all on his own once my mother passed away three years ago. I try to get him to come live with my wife and me, but he likes living in the woods. He came to visit for Christmas when the storm hit."

"The cabin has been very cosy," I say.

Peter nods. "It surely is. So what were you kids doing wandering away from the resort?"

Jamie and I turn to look at each other. What do we tell a total stranger about the conflict we had between each other?

Jamie breaks eye contact with me and looks over at Peter. "We thought it was fun to go backcountry snowboarding. We didn't realize we had gone too far out until the storm came in. Then Candice tripped while we were trying to get back, and sprained her ankle."

Peter shakes his head. "Do you two realize how dangerous that is? You're lucky nothing bad happened." He gives me a quick glance before turning his eyes back onto the road. "How is your ankle, Candice?"

"It's a little sore, but it's okay," I answer.

"When you get back to the resort, make sure you rest it, okay?"

"I will."

Of course I would be resting it, because I know the moment we get back to the resort, I will be grounded. My parents will make sure I stay in the room for the rest of the day while everyone has a fun day out. There was only two days left on this trip until we leave and get back onto the plane, and spend the New Year back in Parkerville with family. I don't know how long Jamie will be here for, but I'm sure he will be a prisoner in his room too until it's time to leave. The only time we will be able to leave the room is for food.

We soon reach the main road, and Peter head towards the resort. I still can't believe how far we had gone. I wasn't even trying to travel too far out of bounds. I just wanted to lead Jamie away from the resort, hide from him, enough to make him lost out in the wilderness so I was able to make my way back to the resort in time before the storm to hit.

And if we had been on the news, thank goodness it was here in Colorado because I'm not sure what I will do when I get back to school, and everyone there finds out what Jamie and I had gotten up to while we were lost in the woods. I don't want any rumors to spread about us. Jamie and I have a reputation at school on how much we hate each other. What will they think of us if we were together? Alone?

* * *

First my stomach does a happy dance when I see the ski lodge, and then it does a twist knowing the trouble I was going to be in when I see my parents. Of course they will be thrilled to see me, but then there will be the lectures about disappearing like I did. I was so not looking forward to being grounded.

Jamie and I thank Peter for driving us back to the resort. We also apologize again for seeking shelter in his father's cabin without permission, but he tells us not to worry about it. He is just glad we were safe from the storm. With one final goodbye, he tells us to take care and then drives off.

Carrying the snowboards, we walk up the stairs to the lodge. Jamie watches me carefully, making sure I got up the stairs okay with my sprained ankle. I got up fine as it wasn't many stairs. In the lobby, Jamie makes me sit down while he strolls over to the reception. Once Jamie had informed reception that we are back, the man gets onto the phone to call our parents. Jamie sits down beside me on the couch.

"Are you okay?" he asks me.

I nod. "Yeah, I think so. I'm just glad we are back here."

"Same here."

"How much trouble do you think we are going to get in?"

Jamie looks down at the floor, shaking his head. "I think the punishments are going to be endless."

He is right. I'm pretty sure I'm going to be punished for the rest of the winter break. I only hope my parents will allow me to attend the winter dance. It's going to be my last one ever, and I want to be able to experience it one last time before I graduate high school.

We hear the sound of the elevator, and look over to see both of our parents getting off. They look around the lobby until they see us, a mixture of worry and relief as they hurry over to us.

Jamie's parents were the first to reach us, pulling him into a hug. My parents reach me next. I get to my feet and hug them. Mom cries happy tears when she sees me, and it causes a pinch in my heart for putting my parents through this.

"Thank goodness you're alright, Candice," Dad says. "We have been so worried about you."

"I'm so sorry," I say. "I didn't mean to worry you."

Mom smooths my hair. "That's okay, sweetie. Let's go back to the room and we will talk."

Talk. That was something I was not looking forward to.

# Chapter Nineteen

Gabriella and Hannah run to me as soon as I walk through the door. I wince a little when I almost stumble over, quickly gaining my balance which only cause pain to shoot up my ankle when my sisters hug me.

"We were so worried about you, Candice," Hannah says, happy tears in her eyes. "We thought that you weren't going to come home."

I pat my baby sister's head. "Of course I was coming home. I just got lost and couldn't find a way back."

"I'm glad you are safe." Hannah smiles, snuggling me close, like she was afraid to let go of me.

"Were you and Jamie in a safe place?" Gabriella asks me.

I think back to the last few days being with Jamie. The fights we had gotten into and then those nice moments where you wouldn't think we were fighting at all. It almost makes me miss those moments with him, but then I remind myself how much I hated him. I shouldn't be missing all of those cosy moments with him. So why was I suddenly missing it all?

I nod. "Yes, we were safe."

"Gabriella, can you take Hannah out to do something?" Dad says in his serious tone. It's the kind of tone he uses when we know we are going to be in trouble. "Your mother and I need to talk to Candice."

Gabriella pulls away from me, pushing her glasses up the bridge of her nose. "Sure, Dad."

Dad pulls out his wallet from the pocket of his jeans. He pulls out some money and hands it to Gabriella. "You girls can treat yourselves to something if you like. Maybe see what they have going on in the entertainment lounge."

Gabriella takes the money. "Thanks." She turns to Hannah who is still clinging onto me. "Come on, Hannah. Let's go and do something."

Hannah finally lets go of me. My sisters went into our room to put on their shoes before they headed out.

I make my way to the couch and put my foot up. Mom sees me limping and asks me if I am alright. I told her about my sprained ankle and that I was okay. My parents sit on the chairs that is on either side of the couch.

Dad waits for my sisters to leave the room before he says anything. He doesn't yell, just raises his voice. "Where have you been, Candice? Do you have any idea how worried sick your mother and I have been for the past few days?"

I couldn't look at them. I couldn't bear to see the anger or the worry in their eyes. Anything could have had happened to me. What was I doing trying to do something so stupid just to get the boy I hated as far away from me as possible?

I force myself to look at my dad. I don't remember the last time I ever got into trouble by him. My sisters and I have always been good kids. We hardly ever get grounded.

"I'm sorry," I say. "I didn't mean to worry you. I swear it wasn't even supposed to end up like this."

"What wasn't supposed to happen, Candice?" Dad wants to know.

I explain to my parents what I was planning to do with Jamie, and what had happened once we had wander off. I tell them about the cabin we had found and spent the two days there until we could find a way to get back to the resort.

"I had tried to contact you to let you know where I was, but there was no reception inside this cabin," I explain. "I'm really am sorry, Dad, Mom. I promise you I will never do something else like that again."

Mom gives me a small smile. "We are just glad that you are safe, Candice. We were worried something had happened to you. And then we found out that Jamie Jackson was also missing. I'm glad you both are safe."

My stomach does a somersault at the mention of Jamie's name.

"I'm really disappointed in you, Candice, for pulling this kind of stunt," Dad scolds. "I expect Hannah to do something like this more than you."

"I know, Dad, and I already feel bad as I do."

"Candice, I hate to do this, but for the rest of the vacation you are to stay in this room. You aren't allowed to go out to ski or do any other activities. The only time you leave this room is when we go out for food. I don't know how long you will be grounded for, but when we get back home I will then figure out what other punishment I would give you. Now, I'm assuming you have apologized to that Jackson boy for the way you have treated him?"

I nod. "I have."

"Good. Now, that's all for today. You can go to your room. Put your foot up and relax. When your sisters come back, we will make lunch."

Without anything else to say, I nod, getting up from the couch. I head to my room where I lie down on my bed. There I curse at myself for doing such a stupid thing.

\* \* \*

"It sucks that you are going to be in here for the rest of the vacation," Hannah says to me later in the evening, where my sisters and I were in our room, getting ready for bed.

"I know, but I deserve this punishment," I answer. "I should never have done what I did."

"Do you like this guy?"

I groan. Great. Now Hannah is starting me on this.

I think to yesterday when we danced on Christmas Day, the spark we had felt between each other. I then think about what Gabriella said about me being in denial about Jamie. But whatever I felt with Jamie during that dance, I no longer feel it. Now that we weren't in that cabin, we were going to go back to being enemies. Just the way I like it.

I shake my head. "Never in a million years would I ever like that guy."

Gabriella looks up from her digital sketch pad that I didn't even know she had brought along. Besides our phones, we weren't allowed to bring any of our other devices. I'm not even sure how Gabriella had snuck her digital sketch pad in her suitcase without our parents seeing it, but she did.

"What were you even doing with Jamie when you hate

him?" she asks me.

"I thought I could make him disappear, but it didn't happen," I groan.

I wait for Gabriella to say something back, but Hannah stops her when she leaps off my bed and peeks over Gabriella's shoulder to see what she was sketching on her pad.

"What are you drawing?" Hannah asks.

I couldn't help but smile, glad Hannah had changed the subject about Jamie. I really didn't want to discuss him, but of course my sisters wanted to know everything that happened in the last few days. That means knowing everything that happened between me and the boy I hated with a passion. I never told them everything because nothing happened between us. Nothing they needed to know anyway.

Gabriella put her pen down and held up her sketch pad for us to see. On a baby blue background was the words Winter Formal in calligraphy, the lettering in white. Around the border of the banner were big and small snowflakes to represent the theme of the dance.

"I have been designing the banner for the winter dance," she says. "I worked on it for the last two days when Candice was missing. What do you guys think of it?"

"I love it," Hannah says. "I can't wait until I'm in high school so I can attend these dances."

Gabriella looks at her as she put the pad down in her lap. "Parkerville High throws excellent dances that you will like."

"The banner looks great, Gabriella," I say. "I didn't know you were designing it. Are you doing the posters as well?"

"Someone else is doing the posters," Gabriella says as she looks over at me. "Miss Fields thought I would be perfect for designing the banner."

"That's great. How did you even sneak your sketch pad without Mom and Dad knowing?"

"I wait until they go to bed before I do any drawing. And while you were missing, drawing helped me to keep my mind off your disappearance."

I smile at my sister. Both Hannah and Gabriella were artists, like Mom. Unfortunately though, I inherited Dad's non-artistic skills. If my art teacher was to ask me to create a banner for the school dance, I would fail miserably. Hopefully when we get back to school and help out with the decorations for the dance, I hope Miss Fields gets me to do something that wouldn't be so hard to make.

That is of course I will be allowed to help out with the dance at all.

"Do you think Mom and Dad will allow me to go to the dance?" I ask my sisters.

"I don't know," Gabriella says. "It's too early to know right now, but hopefully they will allow you to. It's your last school dance before prom."

Hannah hops off Gabriella's bed and sits down next to me. "If you aren't allowed to go to the dance, Candice, can I go in your place?"

I laugh, rubbing a hand on top of my sister's head. "Nice try, Hannah, but I don't think so."

"I really wish I could go to the dances with you both. By the time I start high school, you both will be in college or graduating college."

Gabriella sets her sketch pad down on the bed and then sits on the other side of Hannah. She puts an arm around her shoulder. "Maybe one day we can put together a dance where it can be just the three of us."

"Can we do it for my birthday in April? Like dress up in formal wear?"

I smile at my sister. The idea seemed perfect. "Of course we can do that. I'm sure Mom and Dad will be okay with it."

We pull each other into a group hug.

"Candice?" Hannah says.

"Yeah, Hannah?"

"I'm glad you're safe."

"Same here, Candice," Gabriella adds.

"I'm glad to be safe, too," I tell them.

And truthfully, if it wasn't for Jamie being out there with me, I don't think I would have been able to find shelter during the storm.

With my arms wrapped around my sisters, I look over at the wall that was connected to the room Jamie was staying in with his family. As much as I really didn't want to think about him at this moment, I wonder how he is and what his punishments was.

# Chapter Twenty

The next morning, as my family and I went down for breakfast, my stomach ties into knots at the thought of seeing Jamie. I haven't seen him since we had arrived back here yesterday, and after talking with my sisters yesterday, I wonder how I was going to react when I see him.

But still I replay everything about what happened at the cabin. It was stupid to even think that whatever went on between us in there meant something. Yet all I can think about is the dance and the time where we were sitting beside the fireplace, where I swear he was going to kiss me. It was crazy to even think that Jamie Jackson would want to kiss me. The thought of it made me want to vomit because it's not something I will ever do. I couldn't imagine us kissing.

Ugh, okay. I need to stop thinking about this because it is really making me sick.

When I walk into the dining room, there he is across the room at the buffet table. My stomach does a flip when I see him.

What has Jamie been thinking about since we escaped the cabin? Does he think about what went on between us? Does he want something to happen between us?

That last thought almost made me puke. No. Nothing is going to happen between us. I won't let it. Once we get back to Parkerville, we will forget that any of this happened.

I inhale a deep breath and exhale it slowly. I grab a plate and tell myself that it was okay, and everything was going to be fine. All I have to do is grab my food and sit down at the table. I don't need to talk to him.

"Candice, hi."

I look up from where I was grabbing a slice of toast. Jamie stood beside me. I put the toast on my plate, and keep my eyes on it. "Hi, Jamie."

"How are you after yesterday?"

"I'm okay."

What are we doing making small talk? We *never* make small talk.

I force myself to make eye contact. I wait for my stomach to do a somersault, but nothing happened. Good.

"Yeah, I'm fine. So, how much trouble did you get into?"

"I'm grounded. For the rest of the trip. I have to stay in my room except when my family goes out for food. I won't complain as it gives me a chance to rest my ankle. You?"

"Pretty much the same. How's your ankle?"

"It's okay. Thanks for asking."

Jamie curls his lips into a smile. "That's good to know."

We stand there for a moment unsure what we should even say.

"Excuse me, can I get through please?" Hannah interrupts

as she pushes in between us, grabbing two slices of toast.

Jamie and I take a step back from each other so my sister could squeeze through. She grabs a slice of toast then a hash brown.

Before she turns to walk away, she looks at Jamie. "Are you Jamie?"

Jamie nods. "I am."

"Candice talks about you a lot, always complaining about what you do. I think she likes you."

My cheeks burn and I'm sure they had turned bright red like a tomato. At that moment I wanted the ground to open up and swallow me. What on earth was Jamie going to think after what Hannah said? We hated each other. We just can't like each other.

*Are you sure about that, Candice?* my brain tells me.

*Of course I'm sure*, I argue back. What would my brain even know what's going on between Jamie and I?

I wait for Jamie to say something sarcastic, but he just stands there, staring between my sister and I. I couldn't read his facial expression. Was he surprised? Did he like what Hannah said? Why does he have a poker face? If this was reverse and Jamie was to tell me he liked me, I would be angry. I will make sure everyone, including Jamie, know how angry I am.

"Hannah," I hiss. "Why did you say that? I do not like him."

Hannah shrugs. "Gabriella said you're in denial."

"Well, she is wrong."

Can the ground just do me a favor by opening me up and swallowing me? It will save me from embarrassment. And I'm sure once my sister leaves, Jamie is going to have fun rubbing this into my face.

Hannah shakes her head. "I think she is right. You're in

denial."

"And what would you know about crushes?"

Hannah gives me a look, like I'm forgetting how old she is. "Candice, I'm nine years old. I'm almost ten. I have seen movies. I know when someone looks like they are falling for someone." She puts a hand on my arm, balancing her plate with her other. "It's okay to have a crush on him, Candice."

Without another word, Hannah turns to leave the two of us taking in everything she had said.

Okay, this is awkward. When has it ever been awkward between Jamie and I? We have never had an awkward moment. What are my sisters seeing that I'm not?

"Sorry about my sister," I say. "Don't listen to her."

Jamie nods. "Candice, I know we are both grounded and can't leave our rooms, but I was wondering if we could somehow sneak out and talk."

I stare at him, unsure if I like it where this was going. What is everyone's problem today? "Talk? Talk about what?"

"About us, and what had happened back at the cabin."

My heart beats fast in my chest. A million things were running through my head and all I wanted to do was run. Only my legs aren't moving. They are just standing there instead of grabbing more food and then sitting down with my family to eat.

"There's nothing to talk about us, okay?" I tell him. "Or whatever happened at the cabin. Nothing happened. And whatever you are thinking, it's not going to happen."

Without saying anything else, I turn to another part of the table, grabbing some scramble eggs, bacon and sausages. I grab them quickly so I could get as far away as I could from Jamie. I couldn't deal with him at this moment.

And I think later I need to talk to my sisters about this crush theory they think I have with Jamie Jackson, because they are wrong. I will forever hate him.

\* \* \*

Later, when my family went off to do their activities, I decide to call Allegra. I was glad my parents didn't take off my phone like they usually do when Gabriella and I get into trouble.

"I'm so glad you are alright," Allegra says. "I was wondering why you hadn't texted or called on Christmas. It must have been torture for you to be stuck in the same room as him."

"You have no idea," I say. "There were so many times I wanted to walked out of there. It just sucked that we were trapped in there together."

"What were you doing out there anyway?"

I explain to her what I was trying to do.

"I feel so stupid that the plan didn't work," I tell her.

"Don't worry, okay? The main thing is you are safe. You may have lost your privileges for the rest of the vacation, but at least you don't have to see him for the rest of the winter break."

She had a point. Although breakfast was probably the only time I will be seeing him. Gosh, I hope he doesn't get on the same flight with me when we return home.

Later when I get off the phone, I grab a book to read next. I try my best to concentrate on the words, but my mind kept wandering. I'm pretty sure I have been reading the same page over and over again. All I could think about is Jamie and everything that happened back at the cabin. I shouldn't be thinking about him. Why would you think about someone if you hate them?

I put the bookmark in between the pages of my book and closed it, setting it down on the couch. Grabbing my phone, I pull up Instagram and search for Jamie's profile. He had posted a selfie of himself with a Christmas tree in the background, that he uploaded yesterday. When I look closer, I realize it was the tree in the cabin. He must have taken this photo while I was sleeping because I don't remember him ever taking his phone out. Or maybe when I had locked myself in the bedroom when we fought. He doesn't smile in the photo. Just looks straight towards the camera as he snapped the photo. There's no caption on his photo this time, and I wonder why he didn't write one. He always adds one for his photos. Maybe he didn't know what to write.

I keep staring at the photo, outlining his facial features. My eyes fell to his lips, and it reminded me when we were dancing, and that time at the end of Christmas Day where I had this urge to kiss him. I'm sure he felt that urge too, but we both stopped ourselves. What are we even thinking about kissing? And why am I thinking about kissing him right now?

I log out of Instagram. If only that plan had really worked, I wouldn't be sitting here, thinking about what it would be like to kiss Jamie Jackson. The guy is a jerk. He wasn't worth kissing.

The door swings open, and my family walks in the door.

"We are back, Candice," Mom calls out as she slips off her jacket. Dad closes the door as Hannah runs to our room. Gabriella follows my parents into the lounge room.

"How were the slopes today?" I ask.

"It was good," Dad replies. "How's your ankle?"

"I think it's slowly getting better."

"That's good to hear. We are going out to lunch soon. Make

sure you are ready."

I nod. "Okay."

Mom folds her jacket neatly on the couch, then went to the bathroom. Dad went to the kitchen to make himself a cup of coffee.

Gabriella remains standing there. "Hey, I'm going to go out on the balcony for a bit. Why don't you come out on the balcony with me?"

"I would, but Dad said to get ready for lunch."

"It will only be a second."

I grab my phone and get off the couch, limping as I follow my sister out onto the balcony. I shiver briefly from the cold air as I didn't have a jacket on.

"Okay, so please don't get mad at me for doing this," Gabriella says once I have closed the door, her eyes pleading with me not to get mad with her.

I stare at her, wondering what she could have possibility done for me to be mad at her. "What did you do, Gabriella?"

Gabriella places her hands on the railing, looking out of the pool area rather than looking at me. "I asked Jamie for his number."

I raise my eyebrows, crossing my arms across my chest in hope to keep me warm. "Seriously? Why would you ask that jerk for his number?"

Gabriella turns to me. "I couldn't help but overhear your conversation with him at breakfast. I think you should meet up with him, Candice."

I burst into laughter. My sister was kidding right? Me meeting up with my biggest enemy ever. Only Gabriella isn't laughing.

"You can't be serious, Gabriella."

She nods, pushing her glasses up the bridge of her nose. "I am."

"Why would you suggest I meet up with him? Are you forgetting about what goes on between Jamie and I? Meeting up with him will be disastrous."

"But what if it wasn't, Candice? I have been watching you two this morning. Deny it all you want, but something happened between you two in that cabin. I think you should give him a chance to meet up with him."

I chuckle. "Yeah, no. Over my dead body will I meet up with him."

I turn to walk inside. My sister speaks again just as I pull the door open.

"I have already arranged for you to meet up with him tonight."

I stop. Was Gabriella being serious right now? Why would she do something like that? I turn to look at her, where she is biting down on her lip.

"What?"

"I have spoken to him, and I told him I will get you to come out here to talk. You're meeting him at the ice-skating rink tonight."

"How, Gabriella? I'm grounded and not allowed to leave this room for the rest of this trip, unless I'm out having food with you guys. How will I be able to go out and meet up with him?"

Gabriella smiles. "Leave that to me, Candice. I'm going to convince Dad to let us out. I will tell him we are going to walk around the lodge to search for inspiring ideas for the winter dance."

I wasn't sure how my sister was even going to convince Dad

that. But it was worth a try even though I really don't want to talk with Jamie. Not now, and never did I want to speak with him.

# Chapter Twenty-One

I don't know how Gabriella does it, but somehow she had convinced our parents to allow me out of the room for a short time. An hour is all they give us though to go out and brainstorm ideas that could be great use of inspiration for decoration at the dance.

I still can't believe she was making me talk with Jamie. I don't see the difference it will make. I don't even want to know what he wants to talk about either. I much rather sit to my punishment in my hotel room than be out in the cold with him.

"I can't believe you are making me do this," I tell my sister once we are in the elevator.

"Just relax and hear what he has to say," Gabriella assures me.

"Why are you helping me? I mean, shouldn't I be helping you with your love life instead of you helping your big sister talk to a guy she hates?"

"You mean helping you out with a guy who you are in denial with."

"I am not in denial."

"Just listen to him to what he has to say, okay?"

I groan. She wasn't going to let me get out of this. "Okay."

We don't say another word the whole time we are in the elevator. Not until the doors open in the lobby, and we step out.

"So, do you like anybody that I should know about?" I ask. "You never mention anyone."

Gabriella shrugs as we make our way through the lobby to the outside. "I never felt like I needed to talk to anyone about it when the person doesn't even know I exist."

"Ah, so you do like someone. Who is it?"

Gabriella doesn't answer me straight away as we step outside in the cold, heading towards the skating rink that's around the corner of the pool area.

"His name is August Leigh," she answers. "He doesn't even know I exist. And even if he does, it doesn't matter because he is dating Becca."

I turn to look at her. She doesn't meet my eyes, keeping her head up ahead.

"Becca Walsh, your best friend?"

"Ex-best friend," she corrects.

"Oh. What happened between you two?"

Gabriella stops and turns to me. "Can we please not talk about Becca? Or even about me and who I like?"

I nod, seeing the disappointment in my sister's eyes to whatever she didn't want to talk about. She has never mentioned about ending her friendship with her best friend of nine years before. I knew she didn't hang out with Becca much anymore, but I figured maybe because they were involved with different school activities that they didn't have the time to hang out. I wonder what had happened between her and Becca.

"I'm here if you ever want to talk," I tell her, hoping she will open up to me. Gabriella has always been quiet and kept to herself, finding a love for art. When she isn't drawing, she is making sure she is keeping up with her studies. At school she does a lot of art projects for school events that teachers might ask her to design. Besides art, she loves doing set design for drama. Being on the dance committee, she is also helping with the stage design for the spring musical in April. But getting her to open up about something that has happened isn't easy.

And I wish this was something she would open to me about.

"Maybe after we sort out with what is going on between you and Jamie, then I will tell you about Becca," she tells me, keeping her eyes ahead.

I nod, even if I didn't want to sort things out with the jerk. "Deal. You also have to tell me about this August guy."

Gabriella smiles at this. "I will."

We near the skating rink, which is brighten up by fairy lights all around the rink. I see Jamie standing beside it. My stomach does an unexpected somersault at the sight of him. Why was it doing that? Me getting butterflies at the sight of Jamie Jackson? Yeah, that doesn't sound right.

"I'm going to be nearby, okay?" Gabriella tells me. "Remember, we only have an hour to be out here before we have to head back to the room."

I nod. "Okay."

"And Candice, I know you hate Jamie's guts, but try to hear him out with whatever he needs to say, okay?"

I nod again. Do I seriously have to hear him out? I'm pretty sure I'm not going to like whatever he wants to say to me.

Gabriella goes to sit on a bench. She gives me a thumbs up before sitting down.

I take a deep breath. *You got this, Candice.* I walk over to Jamie until I was standing six feet apart from him, not daring to come any closer to him.

Jamie's lips curl into a smirk. "Come on, O'Connor. I'm not going to bite. You can come closer."

I glance down at the ground before shuffling forward until I was a foot from him.

"That's better, O'Connor."

A cold wind blows, making me shiver. I hug myself in hope to get warm. "So, what do you want to talk about?"

"I have been thinking about a lot of things that happened back at the cabin," Jamie says. "Things that I think have made me change."

"What kind of things?" I want to know.

Jamie doesn't say anything for a minute. When he does, he looks at me straight in the eye. "Is it crazy to feel different, but not knowing why you feel different?"

I bite down on my lip because I knew exactly what he was talking about. The thing is, I'm afraid of thinking it. I'm not even sure how to react to those emotions I have been feeling since Christmas Day whenever I play back our dance in my mind. Something happened between us and I'm glad Jamie has notice that too.

But I wasn't going to admit those feelings to him. And if that's what he is here to talk to me about, then I don't want to talk about it. It's crazy to even think about liking Jamie. I could never do it. We are enemies for life.

"I don't know, Jamie," I say. "I don't feel any different."

*Liar!* my brain screams at me.

For a moment I'm sure I see a brief disappointment in Jamie's eyes, but then it disappears. What was that? Was he hoping I feel the same way as him? He should know by now that he will never make me change my mind about him. I hate him with a passion. Spending two days in the cabin with him doesn't change that.

He turns away, looking at the skating rink where a few people skated. He turns back to me.

"Do you want to skate, O'Connor?" he asks.

I look over at the rink. It was a nice night to be skating under the stars tonight. Christmas may be over for another year, but a Christmas song was still playing on the speaker. I look back over at my sister. She is looking at something on her phone, but I could see she was trying not to let me see that she was watching me. She could watch me all she wanted, but nothing was ever going to happen between Jamie and me. We are just too different people.

"If you don't want to because of your ankle, I totally understand," he adds when I don't answer straight away.

I turn back to Jamie. "I think my ankle will be okay."

"So that's a yes?"

I nod. "It's a yes."

He smiles, and then we walk over to the rental shed to grab our skates.

I hadn't gone skating in a while, and for a moment I thought that maybe I had forgotten how to skate or wouldn't be steady on my feet. That thought quickly disappeared as I hit the ice first, skating around the rink with Jamie right behind me without any trouble.

"Hey, slow down, O'Connor," Jamie calls out to me.

I chuckle. "Not a chance, Jamie."

I keep my head ahead as I skated until Jamie passes me. He spins around, skating backwards as he sticks out his tongue at me. I narrow my eyes at him.

"Oh no, I'm not letting you skate ahead of me," I tell him.

"And why not? Afraid I will do something behind your back?"

"I wouldn't be surprise if that's what you would do."

Jamie playfully sticks out his tongue. I narrow my eyes at him, and then speed past him. Only I didn't get far when he grabs my wrist and pulls me towards him.

"Hang on, O'Connor," he says. "Where do you think you're going?"

"Where do you think I'm going?" I say as he takes my other hand, and we twirl around the ice. "I'm trying to get away from you."

"Not tonight you aren't. Enjoy this night with me, Candice, because you and I both know that we aren't going to be doing this once we get back home."

He was right. We weren't. And even if we did, people will talk. It's not like I'm afraid of what people would say, because honestly people can say whatever they want. I just don't want people to gossip or spread lies. People will think we are together, and that's the last thing I want, especially when everyone knows *exactly* how I feel about him. I'm thankful that our disappearance wasn't broadcast nationally and just in the state of Colorado, because if anyone found out back home in New York, people will get the wrong idea.

I try to remove my hands from him, but he only tightens the grip on me.

"Why are you so stubborn, O'Connor?" he asks me.

I raise an eyebrow at him. "I'm being stubborn?"

"Yeah, you are. Like I brought you out here to talk, but you are avoiding it right now. And here we are ice skating together, but you don't want to do it."

"I don't want to hold hands. I just want to skate without holding your hand."

He lets go of my hand then. "Okay. Well, there is something I really want to talk about with you, Candice."

I roll my eyes. "Then spit it out already, Jamie. We don't exactly have a lot of time before we both have to get back to our rooms or we are in trouble. Where's your family, by the way?"

"They are over in the entertainment lounge. I snuck out here so I could talk to you."

"Okay, well say what you need to say."

"Candice, I..." His voice trails off.

I wait for him, staring straight back at him to continue on and to tell me what he wants to say. But he doesn't say anything. Instead, he reaches out and strokes my cheek. For a moment, it just felt like we were the only two people here at this skating rink. The Christmas music in the background reminds me of the cabin. And that's when Jamie tilts his head towards me.

I'm lost in the moment, and I lean forward the rest of the way. As our lips are about to touch, I realize what I was doing.

I jump backwards. There is no way I was kissing Jamie Jackson. Not now, not never. What was I thinking to allow him to kiss me? It will be the biggest mistake if I did. And how did I know he wasn't doing this to mess with me?

"I have to go," I blurt out.

I turn and skated to the exit. Jamie follows me.

"You don't need to go, Candice."

"Yes, I do."

"Why? Because I tried to kiss you?"

I spin around. "Of course. Do you really think I'm stupid enough to kiss you?"

Jamie smirks. "What makes it sound like you're stupid enough to kiss me? Come on, O'Connor. You can't fool me that you wanted to kiss me, too."

"And why would I kiss you?"

"Because you think I'm a hot, sexy guy." He wiggles his eyebrows.

I roll my eyes. Here he goes again. Being so full of himself, thinking every girl on Earth will fall at his feet. But I, Candice Abigail O'Connor, am not going to be one of those girls. I rather die than kiss Jamie.

I turn to walk off the rink. I grab my boots from the rental booth and sit down on the bench to take off my skates. I have the laces off one skate before Jamie stands in front of me.

"I like you, Candice," Jamie says. I freeze at this, my eyes on my skate and my fingers on the laces. "I fell for you in that cabin."

I force myself to look up at him. I search his face, trying to find something in his facial features that he was making all of this up, that he didn't mean anything he was saying. This has to be all some kind of joke. Jamie Jackson can not like me. He can *never* like me. He is playing a prank on me. I'm sure of it. Only there was nothing in his facial features to show me that he was making all of this up. For once, Jamie is actually serious about what he said to me.

He likes me.

For a moment I stop breathing at his words. I have never had a guy come up to me to say they like me. And at this, I didn't know what to say or how to react. I knew I should be saying something like "Thank you" or "I like you too", but those words wouldn't form. They weren't even the words I wanted to say back.

Jamie stands there, waiting for me to say something back in response to his confession. Why, after all of these years of fighting with each other, would he come out and say he likes me? It doesn't make sense to me.

*Of course it makes sense, Candice*, I say to myself. *You also felt things towards him in the cabin.* Only I didn't feel those things towards him now that we were back where we belong.

And I don't want to ever feel those feelings again.

"Say something, Candice," Jamie says when I don't response.

"What do you want me to say, Jamie? I like you, too?"

He nods. "Yes, I do."

"Well, I don't like you. Okay?"

I take my foot out of the skate and put one boot on, tying up the laces.

"That's BS and you know it," he tells me.

I look up at him. "And why isn't liking you back BS?"

"It is because you're denying you felt anything back at that cabin. The way we dance, there was a connection. Then when we almost kiss by the fire but you pull away, you were probably just scared. And right here, right now, you were in the moment to kiss me too, but then pull back."

I narrow my eyes. Why is everyone saying I'm in denial? "Oh, are you just going to be like my sisters now? Tell me I'm in denial and that I'm secretly in love with you? Well, I got news for you, Jamie Jackson. I hate you, and there is nothing on this earth that will make me change my mind about you."

I sit back down to take off my other skate. I need to get out of here fast, and get away as far away from this jerk as possible. The good part is he hasn't changed out of his skates yet, so I will be able to make a getaway faster without him running after me. Not in those skates he won't be.

"Your sisters are right, Candice. You're in denial."

I chuckle. "Oh, Jamie. You don't know anything about me."

He raises an eyebrow at me. "Yeah? Well, I have known you since kindergarten, and I have learnt a lot of things about you back at the cabin. I'm pretty sure I do know a lot about you, even if I don't exactly sit down to have a conversation with you and listen to everything you tell me about yourself."

"Jamie, you only want me to fall to your feet just like every other girl at school does."

His jaw clenches. "I'm not that kind of guy, Candice. Do you really think I would want girls to be falling at my feet, thinking I would go out with them?"

I get my foot into my second boot, doing up the laces. "I'm sure a hot sexy guy like you would want that."

Jamie's lips curl into a smirk. "So, you think I'm hot and sexy, huh?"

The laces are done, and I look up at him. "No, I don't."

I get up from the bench, grabbing the skates. I walk over to the booth.

"Admit it, Candice," he tells me, trailing at my heels. "Admit how you feel about me. Stop denying how you feel and tell me you like me too."

I stop and turn around to face him. He stands there, waiting for me to say something. His eyes plead with me to say yes, that I like him too. But I just couldn't say it. Maybe I'm in denial. Whatever I felt in that cabin, I didn't feel it now. I can't like Jamie Jackson. I can't. Ever.

And even if I did end up admitting everything to him, I'm pretty sure our relationship wouldn't last. We are two different people who can never get along. I don't want to be in a relationship where I'm constantly fighting with the other person. That's not how a relationship works. And with Jamie being popular and in the jock group, I don't fit in that group at all. Our relationship will be set up to fail.

And what if he was only doing this just to somehow turn it all in a prank later? Make me some kind of fool later on? I don't want to be a laughing stock, being fooled into thinking this guy likes me when he doesn't.

With one hand while I hang onto the skates with the other, I shove him in the chest.

He is startled by my actions, like he was expecting me to come right out and tell him how he wants me to feel towards him.

"You want me to admit how I feel about you? Okay, well this is how I feel about you: I hate you, Jamie Jackson. I hate you more than anything in this world. I will always hate you, and there's nothing you can do to change my mind about it."

Jamie's mouth opens slightly, like he wanted to say something, but no words came out.

Without another word, I storm over to the rental booth, giving the lady my skates back. From the sympathy smile she gives me, I can tell she has heard every single word Jamie and I have been saying. She tells me goodnight before looking over at Jamie. He is standing there, completely speechless as he watches me. I guess this whole wanting to talk to me thing didn't go the way he wanted. Oh well.

I storm past him, expecting him to say something else, but he doesn't say anything. He knows that if he says something, we will end up getting into a heated argument. And having a heated argument right here where the whole lodge could end up hearing, I didn't want that. Especially when I was already grounded, and I didn't want my parents to find out that I was out here with Jamie instead of working on ideas with Gabriella for the school dance.

Gabriella is standing up from the bench she was sitting at, watching me. She looks disappointed, and I don't know why she is. She should know how I feel about that jerk so why would she just assume I should be out here getting together with him?

"Come on, Gabriella," I tell her. "Let's just get back to the room."

Gabriella nods without saying anything. She knows not to. The last thing we want is to get into a fight with each other, and then have our parents wondering what was going on between us. I also didn't want to explain everything what had happened tonight, get into more trouble or even my sister. She didn't deserve to be in trouble. I know she was trying to help, but it's just best she leaves the whole idea about Jamie and I liking each other alone because we *will never* be together.

We are enemies for life.

# Chapter Twenty-Two

Gabriella and I don't say another word to each other for the rest of the way to our room. Our parents and Hannah were sitting at the kitchen table when we walk in, playing a card game Dad had brought along with him.

"Hey girls," Mom says, looking up at us as we join everyone at the table. "Did you come up with some good ideas for the dance?"

Before I can open my mouth to answer, Gabriella speaks.

"We came up with so many ideas, and I can't wait to share them with the dance committee once we get back to school," she says, happily.

Mom smiles. "That's great, girls. Can you tell us some of your ideas, or are they top secret until the dance?"

Gabriella opens her mouth to speak again when there's a knock at the door.

Dad puts his cards down. "Who would be knocking on the door at this time of the night?"

He starts to get up, but I decide to answer it. Why do I have an awful feeling that the one person I don't want to see is the one standing at the door?

I swing open the door and surely enough, there was Jamie. He stood with his arm half way in the air, as if he was about to knock again. He put his arm back down at his side.

I frown at him. "What are you doing here? Did you forget what room you belong in?"

"I just want to talk Candice."

"We have already talked, and I ended the conversation. So goodnight."

I go to close the door, but he puts his foot in the doorway.

"No, you didn't," he spits back. "It's far from over."

"Is there a problem here?" Dad comes up behind me.

"Just some jerk who won't leave me alone," I say.

Dad stands at the door. "Are you bothering my daughter?"

Jamie shakes his head. "No, sir. I just really need to talk to Candice."

"Why don't you go back to your room, son? She doesn't want to talk to you."

"But sir –"

"No buts. Go back before I call security."

Jamie was surprised to hear this. He looks at me before turning back to Dad. "Okay. You have a goodnight."

He turns to walk away.

I roll my eyes. "Okay, fine. Let's talk, Jamie. But after this, I don't want to talk to you ever again."

Dad rests a hand on my shoulder. "Are you sure, Candice?"

I turn to Dad. "I'm sure. Just give me a second, okay?"

He nods and steps back.

I step out into the hallway, closing the door behind me. I

cross my arms across my chest.

"Okay, you have five minutes to talk to me, Jamie."

"I'm sorry for everything that I have done to upset you over the years. Let's forget about it all and start over. I want you to forgive me and to give me another chance."

I shake my head. "I can't just forgive you about everything you have done to hurt me over the years."

"Look, I know I have been a jerk to you all of these years, and I'm sorry." He points to my hair. "Your hair for instance. I know I have teased you so much about your hair, but the truth is I think it's the most beautiful color ever. I was wrong to tease you. I was wrong to snatch that pencil out of your hand in kindergarten. Please forgive me."

"And why should I forgive you?"

"Because you and I know that something changed between us at the cabin. You can say there isn't, but there has."

"So what if it has? That doesn't mean I want to be with you."

He stares at me for a long time before saying, "Are you sure about that?"

I stare at him, confused. Then I frown. "What do you mean if I'm sure about that? Of course I'm –"

My words are cut short as Jamie cups his hands around my jaw, and presses his lips against mine. My body goes from tense to relaxed in seconds. I should be pushing him off me, but instead I closed my eyes, kissing him back, wrapping my arms around his neck.

And then, just like that, he pulls away from the kiss. We stand there, breathless, as we stare at each other.

It's then I realize what I had done. I have just kissed Jamie Jackson. The guy I hated more than anything. I kissed him.

Without saying anything, I hurry back inside the room.

# Chapter Twenty-Three

I couldn't tell a soul about the kiss. Not to Allegra, and definitely not to my family after I had walked back into the room. Dad asked me if everything was okay, but my head was spinning with the thought that I had just kissed Jamie Jackson. If I told Dad, he would totally freak and I didn't want him to worry about me. He has worried for the last few days about my disappearance, and I didn't want him to worry about the guy I hated.

And my sisters would be the last people I even want to talk about the kiss to. They would want to know every detail about it, and then tell me things like 'I told you so'. I just couldn't handle that right now.

My family asked me if I wanted to join in the card game, but I said I was going to go to bed. With my head spinning, I don't think I can concentrate on playing a game.

The next morning, I knew there was no way I could go down to the dining room for breakfast. Not if *he* was going to be there. I couldn't face him right now because all I can think about is the kiss. The way his hands cup around my jaw, how my eyes flutter closed as I wrap my arms around his neck. Our lips moving against each other like we didn't hate each other at all.

The very thought made me sick.

When my family returns from the dining room, Gabriella comes into the room where I am still lying on the bed. With my family gone for an hour and a half, I realize how pathetic I must be to be still lying in this bed without getting up and getting dress, but to be lying here to mope about some kiss a guy as given me. Other girls would be swooning over the thought of receiving their very first kiss with a guy they like. Yet, I have just received my first kiss from someone I don't even like.

And there's these butterflies that I don't even want in my stomach, but they are dancing around every time I think about the kiss.

Gabriella sits down on the bed, handing me a chocolate muffin. "I grab this. I thought you would want something to eat even though you said you aren't hungry."

I take the muffin from my sister, thanking her. I peel back the wrapping and take a bite.

"Do you want to talk about it, Candice?" she asks me. "I know it's about Jamie. What happened while you guys were outside in the corridor?"

"Nothing happened, Gabriella. Just leave it."

Gabriella gives me a look to tell me she wasn't going to leave it. "Okay, so you don't want to talk about that. What happened at the skating rink then?"

I sigh. "Gabriella, the same question is about Jamie."

"Yes, and you always find ways to not talk about him. So please tell me what's up? Did he said something that upset you?"

I chuckle at this. "He is always saying something to upset me."

"What did he say?"

"He reckons that something changed us back at the cabin. He goes on about how he likes me and he knows I like him too. I don't." I give her a serious look. "And don't tell me I'm denying it because I'm not. Nothing happened between Jamie and me at the cabin. We are still enemies for life and that's what we will ever be. We will be nothing more than that. I mean, we can't even be in the same room without starting an argument. And he reckons I should forgive him for everything he has done and said to me over the years that upsets me."

I look sadly at the muffin in my hand. I have only taken one bite and I have already lost my appetite just talking about that idiot. Why did Gabriella have to come in here and bring him up for?

"Do you want to forgive him?" Gabriella asks me.

I shake my head. "No. There has been a lot of things he has done over the years that I just can't forget." I touch my hair. "Like my hair. He always makes fun of my hair because it's red." I put my hand down. "He once said I'm adopted because you and I look nothing alike because of the red hair, which I inherited from Dad. Can you believe it that he would say something like that?"

"I get asked every time at school if I'm related to you, and yes, people do ask me why you have red hair and I don't."

This was news to me. I never knew Gabriella got ask this. She has never mentioned it before. And if I had heard anyone asking her about me, I would have gone off them for asking her that question. Just because we have two different hair colors doesn't mean we aren't related.

"Why didn't you tell me about this?" I ask her.

"I didn't want you to worry."

"Yeah, but people shouldn't be telling you this kind of stuff. It's wrong they are saying it."

"I know. I try not to let it get to me much. So what's going to happen with you and Jamie? Like when we leave here and go back to school?"

"I'm going to avoid him as much as possible. And I hope Miss Fields doesn't tell us to work on the decorations for the dance together. I don't care who I work with, just as long as it isn't with that jerk."

Gabriella nods. "Okay. Well, I'm sorry about yesterday. I just thought you guys could work things out. But I guess it's not going to happen."

She looks way from me with sadness, staring at the carpet. Why would she want me to work things out with Jamie? She knows about our history. Working things out with him was like solving a jigsaw puzzle and finding you have one missing piece. No matter what you do to try and find that missing piece, you can't because it's lost. I could spend my time trying to work Jamie out and forgive him about the past, but it will be pointless because we will be finding something else to fight about.

She turns to head towards the door when she looks back to me. "Candice, I know how much you hate Jamie. But sometimes as much as we don't want to forgive someone because of something they did, in order to move on we have to force ourselves to forgive that person."

I stare at my sister, surprised by her wise words. As the oldest, I always thought that I would be the one to give this kind of speech with my sisters. Instead, my middle sister was the one giving it to me, and I knew she was right. Only I don't know how I'm ever going to forgive Jamie.

"Thanks, Gabriella."

She smiles at me and then leaves the room.

Once my sister is gone, my fingers went to my lips where Jamie had kissed me last night. I can still feel his lips on mine, and the thought of it made butterflies dance around my stomach. I didn't want them there, but they were.

Why, oh why, did I let that jerk kiss me? Why did I kiss him back?

How was this kiss going to change between us? Do I even want to know?

# Chapter Twenty-Four

The good thing was when we left for the airport the next day, Jamie's family wasn't there. I was thankful they were probably taking a later flight. The last thing I wanted was to spend the flight home with Jamie. Next week I will be seeing him back at school, and I wasn't sure if I was prepared for that, but right now I just wanted to be alone without him around.

The flight home without him is peaceful, and I'm sure everyone on this flight would be thankful not to hear us bickering. I still couldn't tell anyone that I had kissed Jamie. Okay, *he* kissed me. And as it was my first kiss, I wanted to talk about it with Mom and share my experience with my sisters. But instead it was with someone I hated, and I rather keep it all a secret.

But of course keeping secrets never lasts long, especially when your mother knows something is up.

While we were at Los Angeles airport, waiting to board our plane back to New York, she asks me to come for a walk with her. I walk alongside her around the terminal, not going too far from our gate.

"Do you want to talk about it, Candice?" she asks me, her eyebrows drawn together.

I don't look at my mom, but I can feel her eyes looking at me through her glasses.

"Talk about what?" I ask innocently. Of course I knew what she was referring to. I just don't want to be talking about that jerk.

"You know very well what I'm referring to, Candice. You can talk to me about it. I know it's about that boy."

"What makes you think it's about Jamie?"

Mom stops next to a glass window looking out onto the tarmac. She gently takes her hand, puts it on my arm and turns me around to face her.

She gives me a warm smile. "I know it's about him, honey. For one thing, when you came back into the room after you went out to speak to him, you seem different."

"Different in what way?"

"Different as you have been quiet. Yesterday and today you didn't want to come down for breakfast because you weren't feeling well. Honey, I was seventeen once too. I know something happened between you and that boy."

I sigh because of course I wasn't going to be able to keep the kiss a secret. If not from my sisters or from my best friend, one of my parents will get it out of me, Mom was the one to do so. I was thankful it was her because I don't think I want to confess up to Dad about kissing a boy. He will be worried and would want to lock me up forever, especially when he clearly says my sisters and I can't date until we are eighteen. I'm pretty sure that even then when I turn eighteen in August next year,

I will be leaving for college and I will most likely still not be able to date. But I'm sure that's just his way of never having to let us go.

"Jamie and I have been fighting since kindergarten over some stupid thing that happened," I explain. "Over the years we would do things to irritate each other. I so badly wanted to make him disappear on the trip so I could enjoy this vacation without him annoying me. That's why I wander off the resort, in hope I could ditch him out there and he will have trouble finding his way back to the resort. But of course everything turned out to be the opposite of what I was planning to do. And then when we were in the cabin, something changed between us. Something that Gabriella, Hannah and Jamie tells me I'm denying about. And when he came to speak to me the other night, he kissed me. The worst part is that I returned the kiss."

As soon as I let this all out, it feels as a weight has been lifted off my chest, and it felt good to finally tell someone about what had happened even if I wanted to keep it quiet. But I'm glad it was Mom who I had told.

She gives me a warm smile, patting my arm before pulling me in for a hug. As soon as I'm pressed up against her chest with her arms around me, I burst into tears. The airport was the last place on Earth I wanted to be crying. Strangers will surely look our way and wonder what I'm crying about.

Mom rubs her hand up and down my back. "Shhh, it's okay, Candice. Everything is okay."

I pull away from Mom, wiping my eyes. "But I don't feel okay."

Mom rests her hands on either side of my arms. "Why don't you feel okay?"

"It's everything to do with Jamie. I feel like a fool for trying to vanish him, only to make things worse for the both of us. And then I find out that he started falling for me. I mean, we hate each other. We are enemies for life. And he kissed me. My first kiss is with someone I don't even like."

Mom rubs a hand up and down my left arm. "May I ask how do you feel about Jamie? You said so yourself that he and your sisters said that you were in denial about him. Are you?"

I shrug. "I don't know what I feel about him. All I know is that I hate him."

"Our feelings can change for someone. We can say we hate someone, but over time something can change. We may not even want to admit it to ourselves. Do you think that's how you could feel about Jamie?"

I shrug. "I don't know."

"Well, I'm not saying you have to like him. But maybe you just need some time to think about how you feel. I'm sure Jamie didn't mean to do something to upset you."

I scoff. "Yeah, Mom, trust me. He always does something to upset me."

"It could be different this time."

An announcement is made about our flight back to New York. It's starting to board.

Mom gives me another warm smile. "If you want, when we get back home we can talk about this some more. For now, we better head back to the others."

Without another word about Jamie, Mom and I head back to our gate to board our flight back home.

# Chapter Twenty-Five

It felt good to be back at home, away from everything that has happened at the resort. But even if I was away from it all, it doesn't stop me thinking about it.

When I see my dad's parents coming to pick us up at the airport, I do everything I can to keep my head held high and to put on a fake smile. The last thing I wanted was for everyone to start asking me questions and I didn't feel up to answering anything. As long as Mom knew what had happened, no one else needs to know. Not until I'm ready to reveal to anyone what had happened.

As soon as we get home, I went to call Allegra to let her know I was back. My grandparents were staying for the day and had offered to prepare lunch for us. Mom and Dad tell them there is no reason for them to do that, but they weren't listening. When we sit down to lunch where chicken salad sandwiches were made, I do my best to eat even if I didn't have much of an appetite.

When I'm alone in my room later, with Belle curl up beside me, I log onto Instagram. Jamie had posted a selfie of him at the airport. His caption reads: *Going home, wish winter break didn't have to end.* I stare at his picture for a long time and the butterflies dance around my stomach. The butterflies shouldn't be there and I want them to just go away, but they insist on staying, making me hate myself as I replay back the kiss.

The next day my parents sat me down in the living room. I didn't have to ask what they wanted to talk about, because I knew it had something to do with my punishment. Mom and I sat on the couch while Dad sat in his armchair.

"Before you start listing what my punishment is, can I just say something?" I say.

Dad nods with his approvable. "Sure."

I look between my parents. "I want to apologize for what I had done, and I shouldn't have done it. I'm sorry I worried you guys so much, and I promise I will never do it again. Also, the winter dance is coming up soon. It's my final dance before prom and I want to really be a part of it. Especially because I had signed up to help with decorations that I had promised Gabriella I will do. So I hope I can still do that."

"Gabriella has spoken to us about the decorations for the dance, and your mother and I have talked. If you are on your best behavior for the next few weeks, we will allow you to go to the dance, but if you aren't then it's a no. We have also decided that you will be grounded for three weeks. For the next few weeks you aren't allow to go anywhere, not even to Allegra's house. You will be allowed to take your phone to school in case you need to contact us, but you must hand it over once you return home. As for your afterschool activities, you're allowed to attend your newspaper club on Mondays, Wednesdays, and

Fridays. As soon as you're finished there, come right home. You're also allowed to stay back with Gabriella when helping with the dance. Okay?"

I nod. "Okay. I understand."

Mom holds her palm out to me. "Can I have your phone please, Candice?"

Without arguing, I hand over my phone. I then head back upstairs to my room.

Well, I guess I can't stalk Jamie on social media. Maybe that's a good thing.

* * *

The last day of 2021 may not be going the way I wanted, but at least later that evening my parents had allowed me to come with them to Parkerville Showground for the annual winter carnival that runs for two weeks, starting the day before Christmas Eve and ending the day after New Year's Day. It was better than being stuck at home on my own. The showground had rides, food stalls, bands playing live music, and later in the evening there will be fireworks once it's midnight. I doubt though that Hannah was even going to be able to make it to midnight. Even though I was grounded, I was thankful my parents allowed me to have my phone while I wander around the showground with my sisters.

"Can we get cotton candy?" Hannah asks Gabriella and I.

I buy a stick for my sister. Gabriella and I also buy ourselves one. We walk around the showground eating the cotton candy. We stop at a few stalls and play games. Gabriella wins a medium size panda bear. Hannah tries to win a giant unicorn, but wasn't able to win the stall game. After walking around the showgrounds and playing games, we meet our parents for dinner.

I'm half way through eating my hot dog when I see him. He is with some of his friends from school, and has not seen me yet. I frown at him. Why was he here?

I decide to follow him. I excused myself and told my parents I was going to the bathroom. I get up, heading in the direction to where the portable toilets were, and when I was sure my parents weren't looking, I dash off in the direction of Jamie.

I keep a distance from him and his friends, hoping he would not look my way. But when his friends stop in front of a basketball throw game stall, that's when Jamie glances my way, our eyes locking.

The butterflies immediately appear and I'm not even sure why. At the back of my mind a voice tells me to run and get out of here, but my feet for some reason wouldn't move. They just stay planted where they are as I stare back at Jamie.

He says something to his friends and then heads in my direction.

"O'Connor."

At the mention of my name, I turn and walk as fast as I can. Why on Earth did I follow that jerk?

"Candice, stop." I hear his feet along the dirt as he chases me.

He grabs my arm and spins me around to face me before I had the chance to push him off me. As soon as I'm facing him, his hands planted on both of my arms, it takes me all back to when we were in the corridor and he had kissed me. My eyes went straight to his lips, wanting to feel them on mine again. But I quickly snap myself out of that thought and frown at

Jamie.

"Let go of me, you jerk," I say, shaking off his hands.

Jamie listens and drops his hands. "What are you doing following me?"

"I'm not following you."

Jamie scoffs. "Really, O'Connor? You may think I didn't see you following me back there, but I saw you. So why were you following me?"

As soon as he says this, I had no idea why I even followed him. It was just something I wanted to do. To see what he was up to.

But I wasn't going to tell him that.

"I wasn't following you," I growl at him.

"Sure you weren't," he smirks. "But you should probably go back to your family before you get into trouble for sneaking off to see me."

He is right. I don't want my parents to know why I was taking so long in the bathroom for. I don't want them to start getting suspicious that I had wander off without their consent. The last thing I wanted was to be grounded more longer than just three weeks.

But instead of walking off, I stay there in my spot, eyeing him. I can't help but snicker.

"Yeah, well what about you, huh?" I say. "You are telling me what to do. Why are you here? I'm pretty sure you're grounded yourself just like I am."

"Yes, so I snuck out of the house to be with my friends tonight. You have a problem with that?"

"No. I don't care what you do."

Without saying anything else, I turn to walk off. I need to get back to my family.

"Hey, O'Connor?" Jamie calls out to me.

I turn back to him. He has a great big smirk on his face.

"Why don't you just admit it already that you love me, and that's why you followed me?" he says.

I frown at him, and then storm off back in the direction of my family. That guy has some nerve saying things like that to me. I will get him back somehow.

# Chapter Twenty-Six

Thankfully I was never questioned on why I had taken so long in the bathroom. I sat back down with my family to finish my food. We then decided to watch and listen to the live music. We stayed until nine o'clock instead of midnight, as Hannah was already falling asleep against Mom's shoulder. She may not make it to midnight to watch the fireworks, but at least she was able to see the fireworks the carnival lit up around nine.

I thought I would see Jamie again after I followed him earlier, but I didn't and I was glad.

Back home in our pyjamas, my parents, Gabriella and I sat down in front of the television to watch the concert at Time Square, waiting for the ball to drop at midnight. Belle sat on my lap, where I gently stroke her.

But I wasn't paying much attention to the TV. Jamie was wandering through my mind and all I wanted to do was wrack my head to get him out. I didn't want to think about him, but it's like all I seem to think about since we left the cabin. Does Jamie think about me too? Is he thinking about me right now? What kind of things is he thinking about me? Maybe how he wished he could kiss me at midnight?

Gosh, I hope he isn't thinking about me. And why would I wonder if he could kiss me at midnight? He isn't thinking that at all.

Before I go to bed, Gabriella allows me to send a text to Allegra from her phone to wish her a happy new year. I also sneak a glance at Jamie's profile before I hang it back to her. He posted a picture fifteen minutes ago, a selfie of himself with the fireworks going off in the background. The caption reads: *Happy New Year.*

I hand the phone back to my sister, and do my best to fall asleep without thinking about Jamie, but it wasn't easy to.

* * *

School started up a few days later, and I spent half of the night tossing and turning, wondering how everything was going to turn out when I go back to school. How was everything going to be between Jamie and me?

As soon as I met up with Allegra at school, I look around, my eyes everywhere so I could make a quick getaway if I need to. Avoiding Jamie will be hard, but it was for all the best. It wasn't easy to avoid him in English, but I made sure I sat right at the front so my eyes were focused on our teacher. As soon as the bell rang, I scoop up my belongings and ran out of the room quickly. So far so good.

At lunch, Allegra and I made sure we weren't facing the jock table. If we didn't face them, then Jamie has no reason to look our way.

Gabriella came to stop by our table. "You know you can't avoid him forever, Candice."

"Maybe. But I'm going to try."

By the end of the day, I went off for a staff meeting for the newspaper club. Gabriella didn't have an after-school activity to attend so she told me she was going to talk with Miss Fields about what she had designed over the winter break.

I try my best to concentrate on my tasks for the club, but my mind kept wandering. But when I was asked to do a story on the school dance, I paid attention. They wanted the inside scoop on the decorations and what we could expect for the dance in three weeks. I wasn't sure how I was going to write the article yet.

I may had done well with avoiding Jamie all day at school yesterday, but by Tuesday afternoon, it wasn't so easy. As much as I tried protesting to Miss Fields about why I didn't want to work with Jamie, she made us paint the cut outs of the cardboard snowflakes. We painted them a pastel blue on one side of it. Once they dry, we will dip them into silver glitter so they will sparkle when the lights hit them.

Jamie and I set a table up in the corner of the gym and laid out the paint. We were given aprons so we couldn't get any paint on ourselves. The table was covered in plastic and newspaper spread out on the floor so we could stick them down to dry.

"So have you asked anyone to the dance yet?" Jamie asks me.

"No. And don't think about asking me if I would go with you," I say, keeping my eyes on the snowflake I'm painting. "The answer is no."

"Why would I ask you anyway?" Jamie snaps back at me. "You will be the last person on Earth I would want to go to the dance with."

"The same thing goes for you."

I pick up the snowflake and set it down on the floor. As I turn back to the table, I come face to face with Jamie's paintbrush that he is holding up in the air. My cheek wracks it and I can't imagine what I could look like with the paint on the cheek.

"I'm so sorry," he says quickly.

I frown. "Did you just do that on purpose?"

He looks at me all innocent. I'm sure he isn't innocent. "I swear it was an accident. I had the brush in the air while I was grabbing something. You just happened to turn at the wrong time."

I narrow my eyes at him. "Don't lie to me, you jerk. You did it on purpose."

He holds his hands up in surrender. "I swear it was an accident, O'Connor."

"Sure, sure. Say whatever you want to act innocent, but you and I know you did it on purpose."

"No, I did not," he growls through his teeth.

He turns back to his painting, putting his brush down. He lifts up his snowflake. Before he had the chance to turn and set it aside, I inch my paintbrush towards him and blue paint appears on his cheek. My lips curl into an evil smile.

He turns, pointing to me. "Okay. *That* was done on purpose."

"What are you talking about?" I ask innocently.

Without answering me, he grabs the snowflake and place it on my cheek. I gasp. His actions were so unexpected that I didn't know whether I should scream. I peel the snowflake off my cheek, where I'm sure a blue shape snowflake will be if I was to glance into a mirror right now. I look at the cardboard snowflake in my hand before looking at Jamie, frowning. He has a smirk on his face.

But before I had a chance to react to his actions, Miss Fields scolds at us from across the gym. "Candice, Jamie, stop playing around and paint those snowflakes!"

Jamie goes back to painting, but I turn, dropping the snowflake on the floor. Then I leave the gym and head to the bathroom to wash off the paint on my face. That guy is an absolute jerk. How can he think he has every right to do this kind of stuff?

In the bathroom, I stand at the basin, staring at myself in the mirror. I snap a picture of my reflection and sent it to Allegra, telling her what Jamie had done. I then turn on the warm water and wash the paint off my face before drying it with a paper towel.

After talking to Allegra through text, I headed back to the gym. Jamie is still painting, and I stand beside him, picking up my brush.

"Took you long enough," he says. "Did you get lost on the way back here?"

I grab a snowflake and put it down on the table. "Let's just paint these damn snowflakes and not say a word to each other."

I dab the paint over the snowflake.

"That's going to be hard, O'Connor. I mean, we will have to talk at some point, don't we?"

I don't answer him and keep painting the flake until we have to clean up to head home. I can't clean up fast enough once we are done so I can get away from that jerk.

# Chapter Twenty-Seven

The next few weeks was hectic leading up to the dance. In between the newspaper club, helping with decorations for the dance and homework, was avoiding Jamie. He is the hardest person to avoid. Working alongside with him on the snowflakes, his name and face was all over the school. We had two hockey games in the past two weeks, but I didn't attend any of them. For once I was happy to be grounded, just so I didn't have to go to the game and see his face or hear his name.

When it got closer to the dance, I was thankful my parents allowed me to go out with Gabriella and Allegra to shop for our dresses. I had chosen a short crimson off the shoulder dress that goes perfectly with my red hair. My sister chose a deep purple A-line scoop neck knee-length chiffon dress, and Allegra chose a royal blue strapless dress. We were all set for the dance, and I couldn't wait for it.

The dance was on a Friday night when the ice hockey team didn't have a game on. Allegra comes over to our house where

Mom takes photos of the three of us together.

"Tonight is going to be the best night of our lives," Allegra says once we climb into her car. Gabriella sits in the back while I sat next to my friend in the front.

"I agree," I answer. "Tonight I just want to have some fun and not let Jamie Jackson get to me." That jerk honestly better not do something to ruin this dance for me. I will never forgive him if he did.

Allegra nods, pulling onto the road and heading in the direction of our high school. "I totally agree."

I glance through the review mirror, waiting for my sister to say something about Jamie, but she doesn't say anything. I notice her biting down on her lip as she looks out the window and I knew she wanted to say something, but she keeps it to herself. It's all for the best because she knows exactly how I will react if she even mentions something about me being in denial. She could say what she wants, but I wasn't in denial. Whatever happened between Jamie and I in the cabin was long gone.

\* \* \*

"As this winter dance is the last one for us this year," Allegra says to me as we get out of the car, "we should make this the best and most memorable dance we have ever been to."

I closed the door and Allegra locks the car once Gabriella also gets out. "Of course we will."

The three of us make our way through the parking lot towards the back of the school where the gym was. We carefully walk fast to get out of the cold in hope we don't slip on any ice in the process. Slipping on ice was not an ideal thing to do, especially if the ambulance would have to be called if you slipped and broke an ankle. It happened last year to one student. They slipped on ice on their way to the dance, and the ambulance had to be called. What a way to remember a dance!

As much as I don't want to think about him, I glance around me in hope I don't bump into Jamie. I wasn't sure if he was already here or if he was still on his way, but I was thankful he wasn't in sight. Half of me wanted to believe that he probably wouldn't show up to this dance, not if he wants to face me. But then again, of course he would show up. He will probably do something to ruin the dance for me. Yet, it's only wishful thinking that he isn't here because he will be. What will people say if the captain of the ice hockey team doesn't show up?

"When we get inside, the three of us should take a photo together," Allegra suggests when we are near the gym.

I nod. "We should! Are you okay with that, Gabriella?"

I don't get a response from my sister. I look behind me and see that my sister has stopped a few metres away from us, watching something or someone. I follow her gaze to see why she had suddenly stopped. I see Becca Walsh and August Leigh standing underneath a tree. He had his hands around her waist, talking about something before they kissed. My heart goes out to my sister just then, and I knew I had to talk to her before we went inside. She may not want to talk about Becca and August, but maybe it will make her feel better.

"Can you wait for us outside the gym?" I ask Allegra. "There's something I need to talk about to Gabriella."

Allegra nods, and heads off without me.

I walk over to Gabriella. "Hey, do you want to talk?"

Gabriella forces herself to tear her eyes away from the

couple and turn to me. She shakes her head. "No, I'm fine."

I didn't believe that for a second. "Gabriella, you can talk to me about it."

"I don't exactly want to talk about it right now." She gives me a small smile that doesn't quite meet her eyes. "Come on, let's go and enjoy the dance."

She starts to walk away, but I don't let her go anywhere. I grab her arm before she can escape and turn her towards me.

"Gabriella, you aren't going to be able to enjoy this dance if you don't tell me what happened between you and Becca," I say. "So let's talk about this before we go in, okay?"

Gabriella nods, biting her lip. She forces herself to look up at me. "I have a crush on August. I told Becca that I liked him, and then she –"

"– started liking him as well," I guess.

Gabriella nods, and then replies "Yeah," in a soft voice.

I understood now what had happened between her former best friend and her. I put a hand on my sister's shoulder. "I'm sorry, Gabriella."

"I told her that I liked him just before we broke up for the summer. And then when we came back to school in the fall, apparently she and August were together. I wasn't even aware that she had started seeing him during the break. She never even told me she had liked him also. Or maybe she didn't like him, and just started talking to him to make me jealous or something. I don't know."

"Have you spoken to her about how you feel?" I ask. "Or even ask her why she had gotten with August when she knew you liked him?"

"I have spoken to her about it, and that's when Becca turned on me. She said I was jealous of her and August. Because

August is apart of the theatre group, she started hanging out with the group too and made new friends. She also made a rumor that I was trying to steal her boyfriend from her. We haven't spoken to each other since September."

Now I understood why my sister was always by herself, and she wasn't just being bullied because she was smart. She was being bullied because of some stupid rumor her former best friend made.

"I'm sorry to hear about this, Gabriella. You know you could have spoken to me about this."

Gabriella nods. "I know. I just didn't know how to. I haven't even told Mom about what happened with Becca and me. She asks me all the time about how she is or why hasn't she come around the house in a long time. I can't bring myself to tell her what had happened."

"You can tell Mom what happened. I'm sure she will understand. She will probably give you some advice on how to move past this."

"Okay, Candice."

"Why don't we head on inside? And try not to let Becca or August upset you too much, okay? Don't let them ruin this dance for you. You have worked hard on getting the decorations together, so let's go and see your creations."

This gets my sister smiling, and together we hurry to catch up to Allegra. She was waiting for us outside.

"About time," she says. "I was beginning to think I was going to freeze to death out here if you didn't hurry up."

I laugh. "We aren't going to let your freeze to death, Allegra."

We headed inside, and line up to get our picture taken in front of the arch snowflake. First we decided to take a picture of the three of us together, then Allegra and I did one together and another one of just Gabriella and me. We thank the photographer and then went off to explore.

The gym was decorated beautifully with a lot of blue and white. The banner my sister had created was hanging up on the stage where the band is. Tables and chairs were set up around the outside. A disco ball was hung up in the centre of the dance floor. The snowflakes Jamie and I decorated were put together as a garland. The glitter sparkles off them whenever the light shines on them. Despite us fighting while doing these snowflakes, they look so beautiful.

But the thing that catches my eyes first that I didn't really remember being discuss in meetings before when we decided on what decorations we should do was the snowflake fairy lights hanging down from the dance floor ceiling. Fairy lights were never mentioned about being used. Whoever suggested it, the light made it more magical.

"It was Jamie's idea to add the fairy lights," Gabriella tells me, like she had known what I was thinking about.

I turn to face her. "He did?"

Gabriella nods. "Yeah, he suggested it to Miss Fields last week."

"The lights look fantastic," Allegra says.

My sister nods. "They definitely do."

I stare at the lights, not believing that Jamie had thought about adding the fairy lights as part of decorations. I think back to when we were in the cabin, how I had told him how much I love fairy lights, and how I always found them comforting. I can't help but smile at the memory.

We decided to get some punch before going to dance. We make our way over to it. Allegra scoops tropical punch into our paper cups with the ladle.

I take a sip of my drink just as the guy who I was hoping I would not hear his voice through this whole night suddenly starts speaking. But he isn't anywhere near me. The music from the band on stage stops playing and I look over at the stage to see Jamie standing at the microphone stand. I roll my eyes at the sight of him. What plans did he have now to ruin this night for me?

He pulls the microphone out of the stand. "Hi, everyone. I just need to make a quick announcement."

I see our principal standing at the side, telling him to stop what he was doing.

"This will only take a second, Mr. Campsie," Jamie says. "I promise."

He turns to the audience.

"What do you think he is doing?" Allegra asks me.

I shake my head. "I don't know, and I don't want to know."

Somehow the knots in my stomach gave me a feeling that whatever speech Jamie was about to give, it was about me. Half of me was curious to what he was going to say, and the other half didn't. And if he even tries to humiliate me in front of the whole school, I swear I will kill him.

"I wasn't sure how I was going to do this," Jamie tells the audience. His eyes scan the audience and the knots in my stomach disappear. They were now being replace by butterflies, dancing around my stomach like it was perfectly normal for them to do this whenever Jamie was around, even when he makes me mad. "There's this girl, and I really want to tell her how I feel, but she hates me. We have had a misunderstanding since we were kids, and we have hated each other ever since."

Okay, I think I'm going to be sick right now. I don't even

want to drink this punch anymore, but I hold it in my hands. I look around me, hoping no one will look my way and know that I'm the girl Jamie is preferring to. But no one is paying attention to me. Their eyes are all on Jamie. Allegra and Gabriella, though, are sneaking glances at me before turning back to the stage.

Should I be getting out of here before it gets worse?

"Something happened over the winter break," he continues on. "Unexpectedly, our families ended up going to the same ski resort in Colorado. She was furious, thinking I was stalking her. Of course I wasn't, and I wasn't liking this as much as she was. You may or may not have heard about this on the news or some online source, but we went missing from the resort on Christmas Eve. We had wander off because she had tried to lead me away in hope I would get stuck out in the middle of nowhere during a snowstorm just so she didn't have to put up with me for the rest of the vacation."

Please, Jamie. Just stop talking. No one needs to know what happened with us.

But he doesn't stop. "Her plans didn't go the way she wanted. She had sprained her ankle and we were stuck in the snowstorm. If it wasn't for this cabin being in the middle of the woods, we would probably have frozen to death."

Nearby, I hear some people whisper. I try not to worry about what they could be saying, but I kept my eyes on Jamie, hoping he will end this speech soon.

My heart then leaps in my chest when I'm pretty sure he has spotted me in the crowd. Our eyes lock and I think I have forgotten how to breathe, or maybe I have stopped breathing. I'm not even sure exactly.

"We ended up being snowbound in the cabin for a couple

of days. I can't even explain what happened. I never really hated her, but I just enjoyed irritating her and making her mad. Something shifted inside me, and I began looking at her in a different way. I'm pretty sure she did too, but she keeps denying it."

He is jumping off the stage now. The crowd moves aside so he could make his way across the dance floor... towards me. My heart is racing a million miles now. Do I still have time to run? Why aren't my legs moving to run to the exit?

"While we were in the cabin, she made it pretty clear how much I have upset her all these years, and I truthfully didn't know I had hurt her. Especially when I made comments about the color of her hair, which I think is the most beautiful color I have ever seen. The color of her hair brings out her blue eyes, and I love gazing in them."

He stops in front of me. Everyone is watching me and I'm too scared to look at anyone, not even Gabriella or Allegra, who I know is just as surprised as I am right now. With Jamie standing up close to me now, he is wearing a black suit with a red tie. It was like he knew what color dress I was planning to wear and put on a matching tie.

"I try to tell myself that what happened in the cabin didn't happen, Candice."

My cheeks burn when he mentions my name. Great. Now everyone knows exactly who Jamie is taking about. Is my face red? Oh gosh, I hope it isn't red.

"But I can't stop thinking about it at all," Jamie goes on. "I can't deny it that I like you, Candice. You can deny it too, but you and I both know that it did happen. You can ignore your feelings, but you know what your feelings want." His lips curl into a smile. "Come on, O'Connor. Tell me exactly how you feel about me."

Around me everyone is watching us, whistling and seeing what will happen next. One side of me wanted to feel his lips on mine again, and the other just wanted me to walk away. But my feet were still refusing to move. I brave myself to look at my friend and sister, both of them smiling brightly.

I turn back to Jamie, my heart leaping through my chest and my eyes drifting down to his lips.

Everyone is waiting for me to make the move. I think about what Gabriella has been telling me for the past few weeks about how I was in denial of liking Jamie, while it would explain why we acted the way we had around each other. I think of the time when I would stalk him on social media just to see what he was up to, curious about his life. Did I secretly crushed on him, but allowed the things that happened in the past to completely take over me and hate his guts?

But then that kiss outside of our rooms at the lodge was the best damn thing ever. I can't stop thinking about it.

Finally, I step forward, cupping a hand on his cheek and brush my lips against his. Around us, everyone is cheering. Jamie hands the microphone to the closest person and then puts his hands on my waist, pulling me closer to him.

"I hate you, Jamie Jackson," I say when I pull away, "but this is the sweetest thing you have ever done."

He smiles. "Thanks. I also suggested to Miss Fields about the snowflake lights. I remember how much you said you love fairy lights. I thought it would be magical to have them in here."

Everyone went back to doing what they are doing once the music started up again.

I smile. "They do make it magical."

"So, I hope you aren't mad that I went and made that speech. It was one way I could get your attention and talk to you. Allegra and Gabriella helped."

I turn to my sister and friend who watch us nearby, smiling brightly, not believing that they have actually helped Jamie set everything up for tonight. It made it clear now to why Jamie was wearing a red tie. They must have told him the color of my dress.

"I'm really sorry about everything I have done to upset you in the past," Jamie tells me. "From now on, I promise not to tease you again." He reaches out to touch my hair that I have loose around my shoulders with curls. "Especially about your hair. Your hair is very lovely, and I shouldn't have never made fun of you just because you're the only redhead in this school."

I smile. "I forgive you, Jamie."

"*Je t'aime, Candice O'Connor*," he says.

I give him a look, but with a smile. "Hey, I thought we had an agreement that you aren't allow to speak French around me."

"Yeah, but I'm sure you secretly love it." He gives me a flirty smile back.

"What did you say to me?"

"I love you, Candice O'Connor."

The smile on my lips grows wider.

"I love you too, Jamie Jackson."

Our lips brush against each other.

As I kiss him, butterflies dance around my stomach. This time I don't ignore them.

# Acknowledgements

I once watched this YouTube video of a workshop Stephen King had hosted. In it, he explained how you can come up with a great idea for a book, but it might not be the right time to write it. That's how I felt when I began writing this book.

At the beginning of 2020, just a few weeks before the pandemic started, I was hit with a bad case of a writing slump. I couldn't write. Nothing would come to me. If I tried to write something, I stopped writing halfway, thinking it was stupid. The only thing I managed to write was a novelette that I published a few months later. I was bored one day, searching for inspiration, so I created a random family on The Sims in hope it would help me to come up with a storyline. The O'Connor family was made. I played around, hoping something could spark a storyline, but nothing happened. I had a potential idea for *Hating Jamie Jackson*, and originally I had different characters for the story, but because of the slump, it just wouldn't go anywhere. It's not until late 2021 did I finally come up with an idea for this story. I remember looking at this site that showed different tropes, and I saw the stuck together trope, also known as enemies to lovers, giving an example of being stuck in a cabin together. Ideas started, and even though I was half way through NaNoWrimo, where this story became the third book I tried to write during the challenge, I began writing. I didn't get to 50k, but I managed to write something. Thinking back to the characters I made on the Sims, I began to write about them. I had a blast writing this book.

I would like to thank a couple of people within the writing community. Thank you to Leonie Rhule for your encouragement, helping me through my writing slump. Some days the slump was so bad that I feared I wasn't going to be able to write another story again. Writing is my entire life, and I don't know what kind of person I would be if I couldn't write. Some days I took breaks, and other days I forced myself to write a little each day, which eventually I managed to write a whole book.

Thank you to Sarah Swartz for always being a supporter of my writing. While I was struggling with working through writing this book and editing it, I enjoyed seeing you post about your book *The S.W.A.G. Code* as you prepared it for publication. Seeing it helped me to stay positive and encouraged myself with my own book as I worked through it.

And thank you to Nikki Chartier for getting me through the editing progress when I was struggling with it.

# About the Author

Jessica Madden was born and raised in Sydney, Australia. She began writing stories since the age of eight. When she was nine, she realised that she wanted to be a writer more than anything in the world. At twenty-three years old, Jessica published her first book *Right Here Waiting for You*. Writing about characters falling in love has always been her favourite thing to write about.

When she is not writing, Jessica is often daydreaming up new storylines, and can be found lost in reading a good book.

You can follow her on Twitter and Instagram
**@JessicaCMadden**

## Also by Jessica Madden

*Right Here Waiting for You*
*The Jet Lag Diaries*
*Silent Love*
*Chasing The Storm*
*If You Had Stayed*

### With You
*One Whole Night with You*
*Every Moment with You*

### I Wasn't Supposed to Fall for You
*I Wasn't Supposed to Fall for You*
*It's All Because Of You*

www.ingramcontent.com/pod-product-compliance
Lightning Source LLC
Chambersburg PA
CBHW020514120726
47904CB00003B/834